Tamara Faith Berger
maidenhead

Coach House Books, Toronto

first edition

Canada Council **Conseil des Arts**
for the Arts **du Canada**

ONTARIO ARTS COUNCIL
CONSEIL DES ARTS DE L'ONTARIO

Published with the generous assistance of the Canada Council for
the Arts and the Ontario Arts Council.

LIBRARY AND ARCHIVES CANADA
CATALOGUING IN PUBLICATION

Berger, Tamara Faith
    Maidenhead / Tamara Faith Berger.

ISBN 978-1-55245-259-2

    I. Title.

PS8553.E6743M35 2012   C813'.6   C2012-900237-2

Maidenhead is available as an ebook: ISBN 978 1 77056 313 1.

Purchase of the print version of this book entitles you to a free
digital copy. To claim your ebook of this title, please email
sales@chbooks.com with proof of purchase or visit chbooks.com/
digital. (Coach House Books reserves the right to terminate the free
digital download offer at any time.)

'The dream of all men is to meet little sluts who are innocent but ready for all forms of depravity – which is what, more or less, all teenage girls are.'
  – Michel Houellebecq, *The Possibility of an Island*

'My mystery is that I have no mystery.'
  – Clarice Lispector

✖

Teenage Girls

There are slaves on the earth right now, actual slaves. There are classes of slaves and races of slaves. There are slaves on the earth right now, birthing more slaves. This is not a dream. I have done a reality check and there are still slaves. I met two slaves when I was sixteen years old. I met them and they taught me that I had to change my life; I had to make it worth *worth*. I had to learn how to make my value instinctive because an instinct for value was all that slaves have.

At the edge of the sea in Key West on our family vacation – the March break time when I was sixteen – I learned that two hundred Africans died on the beach there after they'd made it on slave ships across. Then Cubans died one hundred years later, dried out to death on rotting wood rafts. Blond college girls also drowned in this ocean, after drunk sex that didn't feel right. Key West: the last blot of American land before the slaves thrived or sank in the sea.

LEE: You know what this story is about? It's the autobiography of your self-fucking-worth.

GAYL: Nah. She was just in a learning position. And then she led us like asses into the ocean. That's funny. She should start it like that.

§

On the first night of our family vacation, after greasy black burgers and fries near the beach, my dad and my brother took one bed with the TV remote and my sister took the other, screaming *Stop* when she saw scrubs. It was some hospital show, an operation gone wrong. I told my mom that I was going for a walk on the beach.

'It gets dark too quick in the tropics,' she said.

'If I can walk around after dinner at home by myself, why can't I do it here?'

My mother was slow with her comeback. 'But you don't know your way around Key West, am I right?'

'Yeah, but isn't that the point of travelling?' I countered.

My mother watched me as I scuttled around the room looking for the key, trying not to get the attention of my father away from the TV. I wasn't going to just lie there with them all and pretend to be involved in some hospital crisis. I'm not a herd mentality. People are out there having drinks and dancing. There's a beach outside our window, a moon.

I registered it was strange that my mother wasn't looking to my father for help like she usually did at home. The first flash of a fight between us and she'd shoot this helpless, fed-up look at my dad to get him to say something about me not listening to her. It was as if my mother knew that her words had no law.

The wind was loud outside through the screen and I put on my short jean jacket, in case. My mother had set herself up on the chair furthest from the TV with her headphones of folk and a book about women in Korea that had a black and white photo on the front.

Whatever, Mom, enjoy your dismal world. I'm in Key West. I'm actually here.

My feet had blisters from my new shoes but I couldn't walk down that hallway without running. Beer bottles rolled on trays outside rooms. The carpet was the colour of turf. Our motel was probably supposed to be nicer, maybe that's why my mother seemed so fucking upset. This was a Spring Break motel full of American kids.

I galloped down the stairs instead of taking the elevator and got out at the back, right near the beach. The air was kind of mouldy, still warm. A gull started to shriek. I didn't exactly know where to go. I thought it was weird there was no one around. I sat on the sand, in front of the hedges that guarded the pool. Fluorescent light through them made my skin green. The beach seemed like a sphere at night – out to each side it dropped into a hole. I thought about Jen on March Break in Cabo San Lucas with her mom and her mom's boyfriend. Jen wanted me to have a boyfriend so we could talk about things. She said that Josh was once begging her to do it with him, literally on his knees, because she was holding him off all week.

'You can really make a guy crazy,' Jen said, 'not letting them have sex with you. It's the hottest thing when they finally get it. It's primal, I swear, seriously.'

I didn't understand how she knew when to do it and when to hold off.

The ocean was black. I didn't want to go close to that void. I wanted to read. I was just going to get up and go back to our room when I saw a spark near the water. It was a cigarette being passed back and forth.

I inched forward on the sand. Over the waves I heard clicking, like magnets that you keep sticking together.

'I can't hold it anymore!' a girl said.

'Come *on*,' said a guy. He sounded annoyed.

Then that clicking sound got louder and I realized that it was sucking, then slurping.

'You can stop,' the guy said. 'Let's lie down.'

Then there was no light and there was no sound. After a few seconds, I heard something else. It was quiet at first, but then it squeaked, or meowed. I felt my heart being startled in time to those sounds. Painful, animal crying sounds.

It didn't feel good to be there. I crawled back to the hedges, sweating. I knew I had to go back to our room. I didn't want my mother to come looking for me.

That night, I had to tell myself a story to trick myself into sleeping.

Me still out on the sand by myself, smoking a spark. One of the guys in our Spring Break motel in bathing-suit shorts holding a flashlight on his balcony, circling it around. The light was drawing a heart in the air. Then his flashlight went off. He was coming down to find me. Me there meowing, slurping, on my hands and my knees. I had pulled up my skirt, put my head in the sand. I could still look behind me, squinting, I could look at the guy without him seeing my face. He was half-naked and hairless. He reached into his shorts. There were sparks off his body, flashlights, cigarettes. His shorts came down. He held himself. I was rocking back and forth. The guy crouched down near me, behind me, and twisted my head. I started to open. His mouth was tight like a trampoline. I was pinned but I wiggled my bum until the guy jerked and pushed up into me, somewhere. My stomach got prickly the way he was corkscrewing through. We were clicking, slurping. My father started wheezing. My sister dry-coughed. I turned on my side and tried to start again from the beginning.

I had to keep imagining that I was losing my virginity so one day it would really happen.

GAYL: Dreams, yeah, are dreams. That there was no dream.
LEE: Everyone was once a virgin, you know.
GAYL: You mean a *version* of a virgin. You could be raped a thousand times and still be a virgin.

LEE: Who the hell gets raped a thousand times?
GAYL: I'll leave that interrogative strand to the experts.

§

At the pool on the second day of our family vacation, my father said, 'I like your bathing suit, Myra, is it new?'

I nodded and then I jumped in the water. My suit was fuchsia, a combination of a one-piece and a bikini. My dad used to give me and Jody and Jeff dolphin rides in the water when we were kids. His back had pimples and you had to hold on tight with your straight arms to stop your mouth from going under. It was awkward before I knew how to swim. That feeling of going deeper, bobbing down but trying to stay up, while the dolphin didn't even know how close I was to staying under.

I wrapped my towel around me to cover myself. The sun smacked the surface of the pool.

'I'm going to the beach,' I said.

My dad had sunglasses on, his nose was bright red. Jeff was reading *Astro Boy* and Jody was tanning with baby oil. My mother pretended not to hear me. She was in the middle of her Korean book. It was called *Testimonies of the Comfort Women*. We hadn't spoken since the night before. I was almost finished *Cat's Eye*.

'Be back for dinneroo,' my dad said, his eyebrows going up and down.

I didn't want to pass by my mother on her lounge chair after making such a no-drama escape. I knew she loathed my dad's baby talk.

At the beach, college girls lay in groups on the sand around buckets of drinks, their bums curved up like fruits. Mine didn't do that. I had to pee. Guys whipped Frisbees over volleyball nets, noses as red as my dad's. I couldn't look at their bodies, jumping like dogs. My towel was a cape. I heard them laughing when I passed. There was this one guy near a pool-hiding hedge watching the game, with a walking stick. He had muscular legs, bare feet and a stomach that I could see the sweat on. The guy stopped watching the game with the college boys when I passed. I thought he was maybe selling something even though he had nothing but that stick. This guy had short thick dreadlocks with beads on the bottom. He was black, flawless, shining. I walked for another few minutes on the beach until no one was around. I left my towel and book in a heap on the sand.

The sea was lukewarm; it didn't seem clean. I crouched down low in the water so my whole bathing suit was covered but I couldn't do it, I couldn't pee.

When I lay down on my towel I went on my stomach like the college girls. My bum was a grape. I was going to buy motorcycle sunglasses like theirs.

'Enjoying the sun?'

That black guy with the stick was suddenly beside me. He had on a rust-coloured bathing suit, two front strings hanging down untied. The walking stick was burnt and etched with triangle designs.

'What's your name?' the guy asked. He had some kind of accent. Jamaican, I thought, because of the dreadlocks. But it wasn't Jamaican, I knew that much too.

I thought that he was maybe going to ask me for money. I didn't have any money with me. I was hoping he wasn't going to ask me that.

'What's your name?' the guy asked again. He crouched down at the level of my face. His bathing suit had been wet. It was rumpled and sort of bulged in the middle.

I didn't feel the sun anymore. The hairs on his legs were little C's and S's. He smelled like toast right before it gets burnt. The hand on his thigh was bigger than my book.

'It's okay, girl. I am just asking your name.'

'Myra,' I said quickly.

This guy had a high, square forehead and a very big mouth. His eyes were moving, soft, the lids were kind of purple. He ran his huge hand through his dreadlocks, then over his mouth. I felt so tired. A man had never been this close to me.

'Can I sit with you? That okay? If you let me, okay?'

I nodded yes. I really had to pee.

The guy laid his walking stick down right in between us. Then he took something out of a pocket in the back of his bathing suit. It was a little clay animal, a turtle, palm-sized, with a graph carved into its shell. The guy looked at me and put it up to his mouth. I crossed my ankles and uncrossed them. Then, with two fingers the guy covered the holes on top of the turtle's shell and started playing. He made one high note for a really long time. I rolled over onto my back. The guy began to play faster in time with his rapid breathing. His stomach started jiggling, his fingers were moving up and down like a tarantula. I turned my head to the side. I could see the guy's face from underneath. Then the song ended with one long note as if the turtle in his mouth was moaning: *Here. Here. Heeeeeeear.*

The guy looked down at me. He squeezed the turtle in his fist.

'That was cool,' I said quickly. 'That thing is really, really cool.'

For some reason, I couldn't sit back up or roll over. The guy was sweating even more. He reached for his walking stick and I thought he was going to leave. I really wanted to sit up but I couldn't. I felt the curve of my back in the sand. I crossed my hands over my chest. I thought my bum might actually be like those college girls', the way I felt it right now underneath me. It was stupid what I'd said, so stupid that I'd said his playing was cool. I wanted to just get up and go back to our motel but I had to pee so badly that I probably would've started to run and I didn't want to run away from this guy. I didn't want him to think I was scared.

I stared at the guy's feet where some sand bugs were crawling. He looked like he had an extra knuckle in each toe – the big toe was the worst, cracked in the pattern of a star. I was feeling too hot, too stiff, getting burnt at my knees. The guy was staring at my lying-down body. He had his hand over his eyes to see me better.

'Would you like to try this? Yeah?'

The guy laid the little clay animal on the crease between my thighs, right at the top. My ankles twisted around each other. I didn't want the turtle to drop on the sand.

'Come, come on. Try.'

The guy's lips broke for his teeth, which were white on top, kind of yellow on the bottom. I finally sat up. The head of the turtle was dark, a little wet.

'Put it at your mouth.'

I felt dizzy from lying down, from the sun. 'If I blow on that thing, nothing's going to come out.' I laughed then and said sorry, even though I didn't mean to. I was just hot. The sun was too hot.

'It's called an ocarina, okay. It's got sacred sound. You put it at your mouth and blow.'

'Okay … '

'Try it.'

'No, it's okay … '

The ocarina was warm. I tried to give it back. But the guy put his hand on my hand, led it to my mouth. 'Everyone can play music,' he said.

Then he sat there watching me decide if I was going to blow. I felt my scalp sweat. I wished he hadn't moved his hands from my hands.

'Go ahead, go.' The guy was stroking the sand with his fingers, raking it, making it deeper and dark.

My lower jaw moved around a little. I let my lips part and my tongue touched my teeth. The mouthpiece smelled like caramel. I finally put it in and tried to blow a bit. My first sound was like a twig being snapped. I tried to blow differently, harder, but it was nothing like when the guy had played it. I couldn't make my sounds sound right. There was a sudden cramp in my gut and I stopped.

'I told you I wouldn't be able to play anything,' I said. 'Sorry.'

'You weren't bad at all. You have to give a first try, right?'

The guy winked at me. His eyes were glassy and big.

When I handed the ocarina back, my fingers touched his again. The guy held me there for a second. His tongue licked his lips. I looked down. I felt a smile in the middle of my throat. Is this how you really meet a guy?

Then, I think because I had to go to the bathroom so badly, I flopped back down on the sand on my back, pretending that I was getting some sun. I knew he was watching me, waiting for something. I put my arm over my eyes. I felt him stare in my bathing-suit holes. My armpit was a little nude crease that was opening.

'The sounds you made were sweet,' the guy said. 'You're just a little bit shy. You're a shy girl, it's okay.'

The sounds I made were not sweet, I knew that.

'Come now for a walk,' the guy said.

This guy maybe thought that I wasn't with my family on a family vacation. Maybe he thought that I was a college kid, that I was more than sixteen. I never thought I was shy, a shy girl. It was like he was waiting for me to say yes. To say yes as if I knew what I wanted.

'I understand. It's okay,' the guy said. 'I should leave you be.'

But he still didn't get up, even after he said that. He started pushing his finger towards me through the sand. I felt like I wanted to laugh. But I was squinting and licking my lips continually.

'Come? Yes?'

I was thinking: Girls get scared way too often. Girls get stupidly scared. I was not scared.

Telling myself not to be scared kind of worked.

I stood up at the same time as the guy. My stomach was bloated. I was holding it in. The guy had his walking stick in one hand and he covered his bathing-suit strings with the other. The turtle bulged in his back bathing-suit pocket. I held tightly on to my book.

This man likes me, and my family knows nothing about it.

LEE: You have to let people be witnesses. It's the most human thing, to tell people what happened to you.

GAYL: Nah, a story is visual only. Words are meant to be spit out and forgotten.

LEE: Trauma gets lodged in our bodies. We can't just spit it out.

GAYL: Trauma's not a story.

LEE: Trauma *is* a story.

GAYL: Trauma's comedy. Trauma's got the power of unseen forces. At least then, with your body, you can metamorphose it.

§

I felt like I was old enough. If I'd had my own motel room I would've just taken the guy back to it, not to do anything, not to pull back the covers, not to scratch, not to strip, just to not be in public with this guy.

I wanted to see myself while it was all happening. I wanted to know how different I'd look when I was eighteen. All the girls and guys in Key West who were just two, maybe three, years older than me. They all had their own motel rooms. They had balconies looking out onto the pool. I saw guys and girls dancing out there and drinking beers when it was two in the afternoon. I knew guys and girls slept together in the same kind of bed that I was sleeping in with my sister. I hated how the sheets were tucked in so tight after the cleaning ladies came every day. I felt sorry for the women who worked at this place because I bet those college kids made a mess of their rooms. We'd had this cleaning lady at home when I was twelve who came to our house once a week. Her name was Faith and she was from Jamaica. Once, when I put my lunch dishes in the sink while she was standing there washing with rubber gloves, she told me that I was a spoiled little brat. I didn't understand at first why she said that, or why she spoke so harshly to me. 'You think I'm going to clean up after you?' she said. 'Or your mother? You want your mummy to clean up your mess?' I took my dishes quietly out of the sink and loaded them into the dishwasher. I hadn't ever been talked to like that. I was trying to think about exactly what I'd done wrong. I remember I went upstairs and called Jen. 'Guess what Faith just called me?' I said. Jen cracked up when I told her the whole thing.

'She's fucked up and bitter and taking it out on you,' Jen said. 'You should tell your mom.'

But Faith wasn't around much longer after she called me a spoiled little brat. My mother said she had to go back to Jamaica even though her husband there had abused her. I didn't understand why she had to leave and why she wasn't ever coming back. When I was twelve I hadn't even ever heard the word *abused* before. My mother didn't explain that to me either, what that meant, a man abusing his wife. She just said that in Jamaica Faith had a lot of problems and it was a place that she didn't want to be.

'Canada.' The guy kept repeating 'Canada' as we walked away from the sea. 'Canada is a good country to be born in.'

I nodded my head. I couldn't walk fast because my stomach was cramping.

'I was born in Tanzania,' he said.

I didn't say: Tanzania is a good country to be born in.

On the main road of town we passed by a bar where kids were drinking tequilas and beer at an all-day happy hour. I had my towel wrapped tightly around me, my book under the towel. I had only about twenty more pages of *Cat's Eye*, but I knew I'd lost my spot. I thought it was weird that the college kids weren't looking at us, because it was obvious this guy with the dreadlocks was so much older than me. Coconuts lay on the sidewalk, some of them smashed. Maybe the kids didn't think it was weird that we were together. The guy turned down an alleyway that opened between two white motels, holding out his hand to me. Bushes with spike-petalled pink blooms hung down to the ground. I took the guy's hand quickly but I looked at the ground. Our hands sucked together. It felt amazing. It made me embarrassed.

'Okay, you're okay,' the guy said, squeezing. 'Shy is okay.'

There was a little store in the alley with a glass-beaded curtain in the doorway. A woman was sitting on a stool outside. She had long dyed-black hair that was frizzy on top, like she'd been rubbing it with a balloon. She winked as she saw us.

'Hi, babes,' she said as we passed, her smile dissolving.

The woman wore green stone earrings that made her lobes droop. A thick turquoise choker held her neck up. The guy nodded at the woman but we kept walking by pretty quickly. That woman definitely knew it was strange that I was with this guy, that he was so much older and that we were holding hands.

'Your dad gives you money for trinkets?' the guy asked, leading me way past the store.

I realized how much pain I was in from walking fast and needing to pee.

'A little,' I said.

'Here.'

We were about five blocks from the beach, I guessed, a long way from the last motel. I hadn't really kept track of exactly where we were. The guy was leading me up a flight of wooden stairs. I wondered how long he'd been in Key West. I followed him down an outdoor hallway. I think it was a motel, but there was no sign. The walls were white-painted wood, with holes in the slats. Spider plants hung from the rafters outside.

The guy opened his door without a key. The room was small and blasted with sun. I was thinking that he was going to play the ocarina for me, he was going tell me what kind of music he liked. I stood at the doorway, not going in. Why'd he ask if my dad gave me money? I wanted to be with a musician. This man with big hard brown shoulders, no hair on his chest. He dropped my hand. I scratched my arm. I made a note of where the alley was, the direction of the sun.

'Enjoying the sun?' That was the first thing he'd asked me.

'Everyone likes the sun in Florida,' I should've answered.

The guy was waiting for me to come into his room. I noticed his nipples for the first time. They were black, poking out, encircled by hairs.

'Please come in now. I welcome you.'

I heard the door close and then lock behind me. There were two beds in his room, some clothes on the floor in a pile. The table had a hot plate on it.

'I need the bathroom,' I said.

My heart was racing and spherical. I turned the taps on full blast, locked the door quick. I realized I didn't have my towel around my waist anymore and I didn't know where I had left it or my book. My bathing suit looked skimpy, it was more like a bikini than a one-piece. I heard the guy outside the bathroom door.

'Okay in there?'

'Yo!'

The guy laughed. He knew I meant to say yes. I took off my bathing suit. His hands were so big. The guy's bathroom was exactly like ours at the motel. There were two thick tooth-brushes in a dirty white cup and a bar of green soap that had fallen in the sink.

I was sitting on the toilet with my bathing suit off with both taps running but I couldn't pee. Maybe I'd waited too long. I could feel it almost coming but then it wouldn't come. I couldn't push it out either. His shower had rust around the drain. My vagina was killing me now.

Then the guy knocked on the door and I thought he was going to come in.

'You okay in there, girl? Everything okay inside there?'

'*No!*'

I grabbed my bathing suit and I tried to get it back on and turn on the shower at the same time, and I turned the shower on and got in it when I started peeing, finally. The water was burning. I didn't feel relief. My suit was half off and half on and I felt pain shooting up as I peed. I was too hot with hot water all over me.

When I walked out of the bathroom it took a few minutes for my eyes to see. Everything had gone grey. I was soaked in my bathing suit in this room with two beds. There was incense burning, a spark on the table.

'Open the curtains,' I said. I heard speed in my voice.

The guy was sitting in an armchair right by the screen doors.

'I said I can't see.'

The guy reached his arm behind him and fiddled with the curtains. There was a screech and rings clanked. A white stripe of sun rippled down his brown chest.

I stood there, arms crossed, testing the light, prickly in my stuck-on suit.

The guy's finger drew figure eights in the line of sun on his chest. Tickling. He had taken off his bathing-suit shorts.

I stood there and I was just watching him: watching him in that white line of sun watch me. Then I saw his penis move and I started to laugh.

'Take off your bathing suit.'

There were drips dripping from the shower, drips dripping from my suit. It felt like an army of ants down my legs. If I could've ignored that tickling I would've just taken off my bathing suit like the guy said to.

'Don't you like me?' the guy asked from his dark chair.

I couldn't respond, but I nodded heavily.

'Well, I like you,' the guy said. 'I already know that I do.'

He wanted to do it with me, he wanted me to be like one of those college girls on the beach, bums offered up. But I also knew that something else was going on. If this was simple, or normal, I would've already been near him, we would've already been kissing.

'Come on. You can come over here.'

The guy stopped tracing the wobbling light on his chest. He looked down at his penis. He shifted on the chair, got it into the light. The sun struck a ray right through it. It was standing up hard, hard-bobbing in little circles. The guy didn't touch it, he was feeling how it was shaking.

'Come. Come here. I'll show you how to do it.'

I wasn't afraid at that moment, I wasn't afraid of his thing or of him. But I was just getting used to looking at it and wanting to get closer when the guy leaned back and shut the curtains.

'You don't like light,' he said.

The ripple left his body. He closed the curtain and made the room dark. I was going to run if he got up and tried to touch me. I wanted to run and smash into his window like a bird.

But the guy didn't get up to try to touch me. He kept swaying silently in the chair. The darkness softened around my eyes.

The guy started stroking himself, squeezing after the strokes, squeezing at the bottom.

'I'll show you how to do this,' he said. 'Come.'

It looked like he was thinking about something and then looking at me. I felt myself hard-bobbing like him now, from side to side, then back and forth. My feeling of being in the room turned into a flicker. The walls and the ceiling met in a curve. My thighs pulsed too hard. I felt paralyzed.

'I don't want to,' I heard myself say.

'Come on. Come over.'

'Not yet.'

'When are you going to be ready?' the guy said. His voice was strained. He was about to get up. 'Hey, girl. We don't have all day.'

He was about to get up and come get me.

I had to get back the sun.

I heard the guy laugh as I ran past him: 'Hey, hey, it's okay. I'm not gonna hurt you.'

I pulled too hard at the curtains. A chain of rings clinked and the curtains came down. I crouched in them, hiding. I couldn't see. The curtains got lifted quickly off me and the sun was back inside. The guy was right there. He had a foot on either side of me, his ankles were at my bathing-suit holes.

'Stay there, just stay. Shhhhh. It's okay.'

I was swallowing my breaths.

I felt him way up above me, whispering: 'Stay there, stay. Stay, just stay … '

Sharp wet heat hit my bathing suit. Eyes open, I felt it soak through my hair. Prickles of sun and prickled piss. My forehead fused with the grains of the rug.

'Yeah, god.' I heard him saying. He was rubbing himself fast above me now. His cock was fat and humping the air.

Like a bug I found my book and my towel. The guy was talking to himself, hunched over himself, and I ran.

Down the stairs, the wind touched me and people looked. Everything blurred through the streets. I didn't care. I ran across the sand and into the ocean and dunked my head under. I stayed down scratching and plunging myself like a dog.

LEE: He marked you. That's what he did. That guy know he could sniff you out anywhere now.

GAYL: I don't think you should extrapolate his desires.

LEE: Why? You think he didn't want to fuck her?

GAYL: Of course he did, he wanted to fuck her.

LEE: So that's pretty ominous, whatever, right there. This guy wants to fuck a beautiful, totally naive teenager but he pisses on her because she's afraid?

GAYL: Man, I think you exaggerate. Feminists exaggerate. But whatever. I'm not gonna yet fuck with your rosy vision of all this.

§

My mother's lips were stuck together. It was a cramped, littered patio for dinner on our third night. I thought my mother was mad at my father about our motel, the wrong timing of our trip because of American Spring Break. Not talking over dinner, though, was even worse than her being all silent and repressed. Everyone else on the patio was talking and drinking with fries in their mouths. It was like we five weren't supposed to be sitting together but by some coincidence we just had to be. Being eighteen is freedom. All the kids on Spring Break who were humping in their rooms and drinking from buckets were barely older than Jody but they were fucking and humping and slurping from buckets. I had a huge plastic lemonade filled mostly with ice. My dad was drinking some Wild Turkey or something. My mother rolled her eyes when he'd ordered that and if she'd been speaking I knew she would've said something like: 'Neil, what are you trying to prove?'

My mother was frustrated. Maybe all mothers are frustrated, as if they shit out their hopes with each kid.

'I'm going to have fun on this vacation,' my dad said to our waitress, who was probably twenty, white-blond, with gunked-on mascara. 'Unlike some people who don't know how to have fun.' More rolling of eyes by my mother. Jody got up and left the table. The waitress left too, saying, "Scuse me a sec, I forgot my pad!'

This patio had red lights strung across it and music blaring, half-Spanish, half-English. People had meat and pickles piling out of straw baskets, way-too-big plastic cups of spiked Coke. I think some of the kids were probably staring at us – this family who weren't even looking at each other.

Our waitress came back with a redder mouth. I bit through ice.

'Excuse him,' my mother finally spoke. Those tight two words were granted to the waitress because my father ordered a second supersize Wild T.

The waitress, who had on suspenders over her T-shirt, laughed stupidly. 'That's okay, ma'am!'

I wondered what that Tanzanian guy was doing tonight. Had he had lived here for a long time? I wished that I hadn't run out of his room. I wished I'd just stayed. What would've happened if I'd just fucking stayed? Would we have had sex? We were supposed to use a condom. I knew that much from Jen. She had a stash that her mother had given her when she turned fourteen. 'Like mother, like daughter,' Jen laughed. She showed me how to put a condom on a guy using a frozen hot dog. It was totally disgusting because the thing started melting when it was my turn, too soft to hold the condom right. We ended up flushing it all down the toilet.

'Jesus, Neil, you've had enough!'

My father had tripped or something getting up from the table to help our waitress hand out our plates. They weren't even plates, they were baskets. The waitress was laughing and apologizing and so was my dad. My mother didn't do anything when Jeff got up to help. My dad must've been getting drunk. He was back in his chair, helpless with his burnt nose. Our waitress squeezed around our table in between other people's chairs. I'd never seen my father drunk. His moustache was wet.

When I was running out of that guy's room I heard what he said. My father took a gulp of his drink. My mother closed her eyes. It was like she didn't have the energy to be a mother anymore, like she'd reached some kind of expiry date. *Come back, you little bitch.* That was what that guy had said when I was running out of his room.

I'd ordered a double-decker grilled cheese. Four triangles of white bread were stacked in my basket. The cheese inside was as orange as a pylon and glued over the sides. *Little bitch.* That guy called me *little bitch*. Jody still hadn't returned to our table. My mother's Caesar salad looked frozen. My father was sucking a caramel rib. I took a bite of my sandwich. *Come back, little bitch.* The sandwich was salty and fat. I felt something drip in my underwear.

That guy's low voice, hunched over, his poking-out cock. *Little bitch. Come back, little bitch.*

I got up from the table. The music popped. I passed by Jody at the payphone on the way to the bathroom. She was probably talking to her boyfriend back at home. *Little bitch.* I pushed into a toilet stall. I didn't even make it to lock the door. I was all wet. *Come back, little bitch.* My finger felt up me. I leaned into the door. There were scratches on the walls. That guy wanted to have sex. He pissed on my back. *Little bitch. Come back.* I was rubbing myself. My pink bathing suit with the holes in the sides. It just took a second, I heard him calling me back. *Bitch! Come back, little bitch ...* A thing unfolded and surged up inside me, as if a kite flying was exploding into flames. The stall door banged. My knees went hot. That was a real orgasm! I knew that it was! I couldn't stand, I was shaking. The door helped me up. That was what an orgasm feels like! It happened from hearing him calling me back, calling me *bitch.* That was how he needed me.

In the bathroom mirror, my eyes looked fucked up. I rubbed my fingers with toilet paper.

I passed by Jody who was still talking on the payphone as I went back to our table. I sat down at my basket, picked up my sandwich and ate the cheese cold. My mother glanced at me and finally she smiled.

§

My dad took breaks from the paper to locate us all. I could see him doing it, calculating: daughter plus daughter plus son plus wife. Daughter plus son plus college girl. Girl plus girl plus girl plus girl. I saw him looking at them in their bikinis. I could tell that some of them even felt it when he looked. They slithered around on their towels, hips oiled, bums up. They liked even the slittiest father eyes on them.

It was the fourth day of our family vacation. I asked my mother if everything was okay. I sat on the edge of her chair at the pool. My mom got kind of defensive, speaking too quickly. 'Of course I'm okay. It's just this book.' And she slammed it shut. I saw the cover closely. Five Korean women were standing or crouching against a rock wall. Their faces were blank but they were dressed in skin-tight silk dresses, with S-shaped, high-buttoned clasps. My mom touched my shoulder. 'You should wear sunscreen,' she said. Then she made these little circle movements down my arm as if she was telling me to put it on in a painterly way. I didn't ever know why my mother had stopped painting. I never asked her either, it was so hard to ask her things. I knew she'd studied painting when she was in university and she made probably hundreds of paintings of these abstract, people-like things – smears of red with shadows for features – that were all over our house when I was a kid. It just seemed like one day all her canvases were gone from the basement where she worked. I saw them wrapped up in garbage bags in the garage.

'Myra, I'm fine. Everything's good. It's fine.'

I almost lay down on that lounge chair with her, I wanted to be smaller to be able to do something like that. I wanted to ask her: Why aren't you happy? Why aren't you happy here?

That fourth night we went to this supposedly fancy restaurant, not one of those college-kid joints. This one was called Ralph's. I knew my mother wanted to leave the second we got there because some twenty-year-old ponytailed shrimp in short shorts was leading us down a black-lit wall to a booth at the back. I was just glad it was dark and they had spaghetti bolognese. Our waitress had on a tight baby-T with a drawn-on tuxedo. Her name tag said *Tammy*. She leaned down into our leathery circular booth to take our order. Jody and Jeff and I were trying not to laugh, but my mom was tense. Even my dad was too quiet.

Later, Jody told us that that place turned into a topless club at night. Kids weren't supposed to be there. Jeff was fourteen, I was sixteen, Jody was turning nineteen soon.

'That waitress wasn't wearing a bra,' Jeff said when we were back in our room.

'She had a boob job,' Jody said. 'She was probably a triple D or something but her breasts didn't sag or move at all. That is physically impossible.'

'Her tits touched my meatballs,' I said.

'Breasts,' my mother said. 'They're called breasts.'

'You're supposed to put the tip in their cleavage at Ralph's.' Jody pursed her lips and made her voice go cutesy and high like Tammy's. 'That's it, put it in there, right in there … '

'Her boobs did look weird,' I said. 'Like seals' heads.'

'Gross,' said Jeff.

My mother looked at my father. My father shrugged.

Jody got into bed with me that night and Jeff got into the cot in the middle. I was eating a bag of potato chips, licking my fingers after each one. We were watching a comedy on one of those channels that we didn't get at home. Bette Midler and Shelley Long were pretending to be Russian sisters who didn't speak English trying to get on a plane. They had kerchiefs around their heads and the most pathetic, dramatic-y, sad-mask expressions. No one thought they were Russian but they kept pretending to be, and they knew that the attendant at the counter didn't believe them but they couldn't stop talking and acting that way, in gibberish Russian, looking fake sad, trying to get pity from the woman at the counter by saying that their father had died and they had to get home. I started laughing so hard at that scene for some reason. The sounds coming out of my mouth became wheezes. They were ridiculous as sisters, too close and never stopping the gibberish talk even though they were in on the same dying joke. They were milking it hard, they kept milking it so hard. Tears rolled down my cheeks. My family started laughing at me mostly because I just couldn't stop.

GAYL: She laughs at the foreigners.

LEE: She's not laughing at them because they're foreigners. They're pretending to be foreigners.

GAYL: Foreigners are comedy.

LEE: That sounds kind of racist, you know. I thought you said trauma was comedy.

GAYL: You know what I'm talking about.

§

We made one excursion all together on our vacation. The Mel Fisher Maritime Museum was only about eight blocks from our motel. My mother announced that they were having a special exhibition there about two slave ships that had landed in Key West in 1860, which was the very end of slave trade in the U.S.

'Fine,' I said. 'Sounds happy. Let's go.'

Jeff whined and Jody brought a book. My dad was the sulkiest, trailing behind.

In the first room of the museum, before the slave-ship exhibition, there were these pieces of wood set up like a sculpture. It was a broken raft, I read, that thirty Cubans had used trying to get across the ocean from Cuba all the way to Key West. This had happened seventeen years ago. All of them died. They'd even found some kid's T-shirt attached to the raft's pole like a sail. Those were the actual pieces of wood that people died on that were displayed. There was a rope around the raft but two kids were climbing on it, their parents totally oblivious. Jeff and Jody hadn't even stopped to see this thing. I think Jody went to go use the phone. Jeff was probably going to go through the entire museum as fast as he could. I was the only one who stopped to look at the raft. Kids our age had died on it. It was a fucking memorial!

'You better get off that,' I said to the kids.

They both had sand on their feet and dirty flip-flops. They ran to their mother and whispered in her ear. The mother glared at me. Fucking fuck you, I thought. Your kids are playing on a grave.

My mom poked her head out from the other room. 'You have to come see this,' she said.

It wasn't right that that raft was out there for everyone to touch, for kids to climb on with their dirty little feet. People should take the time to think about what that rotting thing was. It was a death boat for thirty people. I didn't even have time to deal with what I was thinking. My mother kept calling me out of myself. She wanted to show me a picture, the first picture from the slave-ship exhibition. 'This is unbelievable,' she said. 'Myra, you have to see this, this is unbelievable.' I cringed at how fast she was talking. Why unbelievable? This all actually happened! Why is this all so hard to believe?

The Last of the Slave Ships was stencilled on a white wall. There was a detailed, life-size drawing of a really sad-looking African man with a chain around his ankle that looked like it had been photocopied onto the wall. You couldn't really see his eyes, they were almost slit shut. It was grotesque. Why'd that have to be life-size?

'Myra! Come here.' My mother called me from around the corner, where she stood in front of a tiny ink print.

The picture, you had to really look at it close up, showed a boatload of smashed-together people with cuffs and chains around their ankles. They were all black, bony, made out of criss-crosses.

'Unbelievable,' my mom said again.

I wanted to take this precious grainy little picture off the wall and stomp on the glass and knee-break its frame. Who the fuck was the artist who could draw so realistically, actually set up an easel and draw people's bones and chains for hours, draw for hours each little criss-cross on people who were crying beside buckets of slop? Who the fuck was the artist who worked on that to get it all so realistic? And why was my mom saying it was unbelievable?

People are *like* this. This *happened*, I wanted to scream at her. This is *not* unbelievable at all.

I looked that picture in the eyes. I wanted to see that dread-locked guy again. I wanted to be with him, stay with him, let him do whatever he wanted to me in that room.

My mother had moved on. 'Oh my god,' I heard her whisper at the next picture. My mother started to cry. I hated this museum. Who thought that this exhibition was a good idea? It was exploitative. I wanted to stencil that on the walls: *Slavery Is Fucking Exploitation!*

My father, pathetic, hadn't come inside the museum at all. He'd yelled at the woman at the front desk because at our motel it said there was a family price for the museum on weekdays but when we got there that woman said they weren't taking any coupons. My father said something like, 'What kind of business are you running?' And my mom said to the woman, 'It's fine, it's okay.' Then my father snapped at her, 'Irene, don't undermine me!' It was totally embarrassing that they were having a fight in public over five fucking dollars. The woman at the front desk stared at us like we were the worst kind of tourists, the kind who shouldn't even be at a serious museum. My mother ended up giving her the extra money so we could just go. My dad had wanted to rent mopeds and drive to Key Largo, saying that I'd go on the back of his bike, Jeff could go on my mom's and Jody could ride her own because she was pretty much nineteen. My mom thought that mopeds were dangerous and she wasn't riding one and neither were we.

My mother had moved to the second-last picture of the exhibition, blowing her nose. I noticed that there was a security guard sitting on a stool in the corner. He had acne on his cheeks and his hair was slicked back, like an eagle's crest. In the etching that my mother was standing in front of there were four women, naked, with short dark hair and hanging breasts. They were on the deck of a ship. The card on the wall said: *The Wild-fire, 1868. Artist Unknown*. I was sweating. My thighs rubbed each other under my skirt.

'Myra, I think I've had enough. This is phenomenal. It's making me feel funny. I'll wait for you outside.'

My mom's eyes were all red. I watched her walk quickly out of the room. The security guard watched her too. I thought maybe he was Cuban. Maybe that's why he worked here. Maybe he told people his story, maybe he knew one of the people who'd drowned seventeen years ago. He looked at me and shrugged his shoulders. I thought he was thinking my mom couldn't take it. I shrugged my shoulders back at him. Then I looked at the very last etching on the wall. It was a child, close-up, with a bloated gut. That security guard's eyes were too big for his face, he had really thick eyebrows too. The child's eyes were not sad. The anonymous fucking artist who drew that child's eyes not sad, but really open, with a criss-crossed reflection of a sail inside, made him actually look happy, or peaceful. That child was beside a bucket of slop, in chains. That child was a slave.

'They say there are these unmarked graves, like, out at Higgs Beach of these people.'

The security guard was behind me, looking at the picture with me. His breath smelled like bread. I was breathing in time.

'They do a ceremony out there, every year, where the slaves were buried. An African guy, like, a priest or something, he comes every year special to do that and it's a big party, like, lots of drumming and music, a fire.'

Maybe this guy liked the way I looked from behind. Maybe he wanted to make love to me too. I wanted to make love to the Tanzanian guy.

'You wanna meet me there? It's, like, a big party, we could dance. You look like you like to dance, yeah?'

I turned quickly, shaking my head no and left the room. I knew the guard thought I ran out of that room like my mom.

This time, in the stall of a bathroom that was designed like a boat, I knew exactly what I was doing. I pulled up my skirt and sat down on the toilet. I used both my hands. I was thinking of the security guard out there, outside the door, imagining he was going to come in in a second and call me *bitch*. *Don't run away, little bitch. Come back, little bitch.* He'd have his knees on either side of me and he'd hold the door with his back and hold me in front of the toilet and take down his pants and show me his thing and he'd say *Come on, bitch, stay with me, bitch. Bitch* was a compliment. That child was a slave. I felt it bigger inside me this time, coming like a parachute opening. I felt it pulsing and rising up even in my throat. *Bitch.* My mother couldn't take it. This time I spasmed throughout my whole self.

My family was waiting outside of the museum for me in the sun.

'Where were you?' Jeff said. He looked worried. My father had his back turned.

'Myra, we're going for lunch now,' my mom said carefully. 'Something light.'

Maybe she thought I'd just puked. Adolescent girls like to puke.

'What do you feel like?' Jeff asked me, trying to make things better.

'I don't care,' I said.

'I want a Coke,' Jody said.

'Hamburgers okay?'

'Hot dog,' I said, thinking about my mouth.

As we walked towards the beach to one of those crappy beachside BBQ shacks, I realized that I was really the only one in my family who could handle looking at those pictures. I saw those slaves for what they really were: people caught in a horror show. Men were now wanting something from me too. Having an orgasm was like this private transmission of what their wanting did to me.

GAYL: I like the way she mixes it all up and pulls it all together. I didn't get to see that exhibition. But, you know, it sets a nice tone for our abject adventure.

LEE: You're so critical. You're being mocking, right?

GAYL: No. It's for real.

LEE: I don't believe you.

GAYL: A smart female has got to be critical, you better believe that.

LEE: I do. I believe that. But you don't have to be a bitch.

GAYL: Why not? Bitches are the best.

§

By day five of our vacation, I was masturbating every time I went to pee. By day five of our vacation I was always wet. I felt it walking and sitting down too. I felt it the very first thing in the morning. On day five of our vacation, I knew I had to go back to his room.

I walked through the same alley where I'd walked with him last. I promised myself I was going to stay there this time. I was going to stay there this time and lie down on his bed. I was going to stay so he could take off my clothes. I didn't know what he'd think of me naked, without my bathing suit. *Come back, little bitch.* The only person who'd ever touched my breasts was the woman who'd fitted me for my first bra and she had scolded me for not coming sooner. She'd picked up my breasts and then kind of let them go roughly. She said to my mother outside the change room: 'Her breasts are going to sag. You should've come sooner.' I thought that that guy would suck my breasts. Masturbating felt amazing. I mean, why would someone be afraid of sex? Sex was going to feel amazing. Sex was going to blow my mind. Sex with that guy was going to make me want it more and more and more and more.

I got to the motel with this plan in my head, but then all I could do was stand there outside. Count the rows of black holes studding up the white walls. This time I didn't have a towel or a book to hold on to. I had a one-hundred-dollar American bill in my pocket that my father had given me on the first day of our vacation.

The way the stairs creaked I felt sweat in my shoes. Weeds were growing between the splinters. One of the spider plants had fallen down. Its pot was cracked and the roots were exposed.

There was a room-service tray outside his door – two plates and a glass with milk glued around the bottom. I stood at the railing and looked out at the sea. It wasn't far. In Key West the sea was never far. The guy said he was born in Tanzania. I'd pissed on my bathing suit inside his shower. I'd seen him touching himself through the dark.

This time, I was wearing underwear. This time, I had on a bright pink thong. The fabric was sticking to me under my skirt. I didn't put gloss on my lips so they were dry. I heard a baby crying on the beach.

I knew this guy wanted to see me again.

I put my ear to the door. The door was opposite the bed. I was going to knock but then I heard music. He was playing that ocarina again. It made me remember that we were really going to have sex. That sound was like code for sex, it was the way that we'd met. He'd be so happy that I came back. This time I wouldn't run away. I was finally going to have sex. With a man, a musician, a genius musician. I was going to surprise him. I was going to make him the happiest person alive! I held the door-knob. My hands were sweating. He'd make me come like I made myself come.

The door was open. His door was already open. He sat on the bed, his humped back knotted with nodes for the spine. My heart was racing: I'd let that person inside me.

I slipped half into the room holding on to the door. The curtains were still in a heap at the window from how I'd ripped them down. The music didn't sound smooth; notes jerked, one way up. I stood in that dull dead space at the door unable to move. I heard water run.

Then a woman came out from the bathroom.

She was holding a rag between her legs. She wore a man-sized white robe. The woman was tall and older and black like him, her hair in two thick French braids merged at the back. She moved in a swagger like she was drunk, pushing between her legs and laughing. The cloth she was holding down there was smeared with blood.

'You gonna help me or what?'

I'd come here to have sex with this guy. The woman stood over him holding her gut. He didn't take the ocarina out of his mouth.

'Hey, Elijah! It's the only way to cure this fucking thing.'

The guy still didn't respond. His name was Elijah. He blew a high note up towards her face. The woman started this kind of wobbly dance, cleaning herself with the bloody cloth. Her robe came open and I saw her breasts. They were long at the top and sloped into bells, with dark brown nipples right at the centre. Flesh shook on her legs; they seemed musical too, like a chiming instrument that you hit with a stick. The guy, Elijah, played faster now, following her shaking body with sounds. The room was humid with messed-up sheets and old sun. When the woman got into the bed, she smoothed down her robe like wings at her sides. Her thighs were relaxed. There was no more blood.

'Touch it,' she said. 'Touch me, come on.'

Elijah didn't move from the edge of the bed. 'I fucked up,' he said. 'We gotta leave.'

'With a chick?' That woman glared at him. Elijah didn't answer. 'Fucking please say no. Do I look like I'm in any shape to be travelling right now?'

The woman grabbed the sheets from the middle of the bed and tried to cover herself. 'Don't even fucking tell me if you fucked up. It's Spring Break, right? There's a fucking spread of eager legals. Don't even fucking tell me.'

Elijah tried to wrestle the covers away from her. She was angry, though, trying to get away from him and keep covering herself. Then Elijah's hand gripped her thigh. Veins bulged in his arm and he began kneading her there. She sort of settled down when he started that. I couldn't see it all but I knew where he was going when he kneaded higher and higher on her thigh, his hand using a hook-shaped push. I felt it too. I wanted to feel that too. After a few pushes of him doing that hard and her closing her eyes and spreading her thighs, it looked like he was inside her with his whole arm. The woman started to cry these amazing sex sounds. I couldn't believe she was feeling so much. Then Elijah leaned down and put his mouth on her there. He had both hands on both her thighs, kneading. His mouth opened and he started moving his head between her legs. I saw his pink tongue through the thicket of his hair. The woman gripped his head and pumped up. Then she thrashed and grunted. God, I wanted that too. She was bucking up into his face, like using his head to masturbate. It was as if the two of them were a freakish machine:

he pushed in and she bucked up. Then she roared, it was massive, like a standing-up bear. Elijah stopped moving. After a few seconds the woman started laughing. She rubbed her eyes and pushed him away.

Elijah sat up and looked at her. Her skin was glowing like the moon.

'Don't do that to anyone else,' she said quietly. 'Got it?'

'Yeah,' Elijah said, wiping his mouth. 'Yeah, G., sure. My mouth is all yours.'

The two of them stared at each other. I stepped backwards, sweating, intending to leave, but I pressed against the door and it clicked. The woman looked at the door.

'What?' I said, louder than I meant to.

The woman looked at me. I noticed her bottom lip was split, as if she'd bitten through it. I saw blood on her robe in the shape of a lake.

Elijah walked over to me and grabbed my wrist. I didn't know if he was mad. I didn't even know if there was a secret between us. He looked back at the woman on the bed and kind of moved himself over so she could see me.

'Fucking hell, E. What the fuck kind of little baby is that?'

'I tried to tell you,' he said. 'But she came on her own.'

I wanted him to touch more than my wrist. I wanted him to touch my chin and open my jaw so I'd speak. He should do to me what he did to her. I wished, god, I wished. The woman leaned forward and laughed. It was like she heard my thoughts. A draft froze through my chest.

'What?' I said for the second time.

'What, what?' the guy said, mocking me.

'She's fucking jailbait, E.'

Then Elijah pushed me against the shut door. It was rough and I got scared. My eyes flew down to his grey cracked-up feet.

'How old are you?' he whispered in my face. 'Say eighteen.'

I heard the woman laughing on the bed. She clutched her gut. Elijah had me trapped. He smelled like smoke and caramel.

I felt his eyes on my T-shirt that was too tight across my tits. I stayed as still as I could while he pushed his chest up against me. The woman wouldn't stop laughing, then coughing. It was wrong, it was like she couldn't stop her own sounds.

'Does she need a doctor?' I whispered. I was so turned on being held there at the door by this guy, but I also felt like I was going to throw up.

'Get her fucking out of here!'

That woman had bolted up from the bed. She was staggering towards us, breasts eye-like, alive. Elijah peeled himself off me and left me exposed. This woman was two heads taller than me.

'What the fuck is this, Elijah?' The woman was angry. Her body gave heat, I felt it, purplish, fluorescent. 'Why do you like this baby-faced one?'

I knew I stared at her one second too long.

The woman slapped me hard on the cheek.

'Is she going to wake up or what?'

The woman smiled after she slapped me, like it relieved her of being angry. She walked backwards. I held my face. Wake up? I was shaking. You can't just slap someone for fucking staring. I hated her. I was not a baby. I was totally awake! I was going to fuck her boyfriend endlessly.

Elijah took me by the shoulders and opened the door.

'It's time for you to go now,' he said.

'Go? Go where?' Pain flared in my cheek.

He was forcing me outside. I wanted to push back against him. It wasn't my fault what he had done, how much he liked me. I didn't know that he was with her. You can't just slap someone you don't know. It wasn't fair the way that woman, that fucking bitch, came at me. *She* had to wake the fuck up, not me! I wanted to push back against Elijah and say something right, like: I'm old *enough*. But I couldn't let go of my burning cheek. That woman looked like she hated me. She'd hit me so hard.

'You have to go, angel.' Elijah was looking at my body.

Angel? I'd dressed up on purpose to be his little bitch.

'You have to go now, come on. I'll see you soon.'

'But we're leaving tomorrow!'

Elijah shut the door. The wind wrapped tight around my temples. It made the palms shake. I took the one-hundred-dollar bill out of my pocket and I shoved it in under the crack of the door. Open up! I kicked the door. I am old enough, you fucking asshole! I'm not jailbait!

The sun burnt my scalp. I felt my scalp sting.

I thought about going home, I thought about Jen. She always got sex and I didn't even get near it. I got pissed on by a guy, this beautiful African guy.

I went to that room to have sex with that man.

I didn't want anyone ever to know I'd been hit.

LEE: Myra, you need to explain why you even wanted to stay with him. That woman was horrible to you, she slapped you, and that guy had no balls to stand up to her and protect you.

GAYL: I was in pain, okay? My man fucked up my work. Serious work. You don't have any sympathy for that?

LEE: None of that was Myra's fault.

GAYL: No?

LEE: No.

GAYL: Well, she was marked now, for sure. Not by his piss, but my slap.

§

On the last night of our family vacation, I woke up, too hot, to my parents' synchronized breathing. My father had a pinched nose so it sounded like an exaggeration. He was the conductor. My mother slept between my father and the wall. My brother had the cot. I was in the queen-sized bed with my sister. Something, it was obvious, was wrong with my face. It felt like my cheek had exploded on the pillow. My mother noticed how red it had been yesterday when I found my way back to the pool.

'You got too much sun there,' she said, glaring over her sunglasses.

I knew I had to get up out of bed and check out what was going on. It was way too dark inside our room. My father had shut the curtains before bed because the college kids at the motel had been staying up all night. Our thick flowered drapes didn't hide noise very well. Our room faced the pool. That pool was slimy with sunscreen and saliva. Sometimes garbage was floating on it in the morning. My mom said we'd never stay at a place like this again.

I got out of bed as quiet as I could and touched along the wall to the crack of light from the bathroom. I knew something was wrong from that wetness on my pillow, but at first, in the mirror, I didn't think it was me – my cheek was completely swollen as if plastic were inside it. My eye above it was a slit. My nostril was even pinched on that side.

I realized that it had been me who was wheezing out there, not my father.

I climbed into the tub to lie down. I pulled the shower curtains tight to each end. I felt sand through my pyjamas from all of our feet. Five bathing suits drooped on the string near the ceiling. Mine was that fucking pink wet one with holes in the sides.

I thought I was definitely going to have to tell my mom what had happened to me. She'd probably want to call the police. My cheek throbbed. It was assault. I wished I could tell her what had happened to me, but the story felt too twisted. I'd already made so many wrong moves.

I fell asleep in the bath like the Elephant Man, knowing I would not tell the truth.

§

It was Jody who found me in the morning. 'Something's wrong with Myra, Mom, come!'

My mother's face hung over the bath. She told Jody to get some ice wrapped up in a towel. She was more animated than I'd seen her all week.

'Myra, the sun, oh the sun, the terrible sun.'

She swirled the tip of her finger onto my burning-hot cheek. The fluorescent lights buzzed. Jody found ice.

'You didn't put on sunscreen, Myra, I'm sorry. It's monstrous, this sun.'

My mother didn't want to leave me alone when she saw me like that in the morning so swollen and sore. I told her she should go out and have her last day, I was *fine*. Our plane took off at ten o'clock at night.

'I'm not going anywhere. I'm going to stay here with you,' my mother said.

'Please just go,' I moaned. I was still in the bath. 'Go to the beach, bitch … '

Jody dumped the rest of the ice in the sink and she left the room. I heard Jeff laugh outside. The TV was on.

'Myra!'

I had just said the word *bitch*. My father came to watch me and my mom through the crack in the bathroom door. He tried hard not to look at my ballooned-up cheek.

'Myra,' my mom said softly. 'Why are you so upset?'

'Why the fuck do you think I'm upset?' I swore really loud. My mom stepped backwards. It flew out of my mouth, first *bitch* and now *fuck*.

'Myra!' my dad yelled. 'Quiet!'

I noticed Jody and Jeff go out to the hallway. 'Take the kids to the beach, Neil. Please.'

I got out of the bathtub and ran past my mother, then my father, to the chairs near the window. I was mad and it felt good.

'She is not coming anywhere with us,' my dad said to my mom. My dad's eyes were alive, like the lids were peeled back. I tried to stay still. He was never really that nice to my mom; he never asked about her, or about what was she thinking. Now he was trying to defend her against me. It was a total joke. Even my mom knew that. I wasn't going to the beach, anyway, looking like a freak. My dad's too-open eyes made me queasy and hateful.

'I just want to be alone, all right?'

'Neil, go. We don't need you right now.'

It took a minute before he left, before he tried to slam the door shut even though it was on one of those non-slammable hinges. We heard him say *goddammit* in the hall. My mom walked over to me near the air conditioning. She had to fiddle around with it to stop it.

'Fuck this thing,' she said. She looked out the window. Three guys were doing cannonballs into the pool.

When my mom looked at me again, my big red fat cheek, I thought she was going to say something like, 'I think you should try not talking to me like that.'

But I heard my mother breathing too fast. She kissed me on the forehead.

'Bye-bye,' she whispered as if I were a baby. Her breath was sour. My throat instantly swelled. My mother stayed close to me like that, not moving. I wanted to apologize: *Bitch* just flew out of me. I met this guy who called me *bitch* …

I heard my mom swallow inside her throat. I was staring at the floor watching her feet. For a while I didn't think she was going to leave.

'Can you go now?' I asked.

My mother moved away. I knew I didn't sound nice. I stared through the screen doors at the kids at the pool, their burnt red shoulders, their string bikinis. The palm trees were waving, dry at the tips. When I heard the door click, I couldn't believe that my mother had listened to me.

I had the TV to myself. My cheek was really hurting. I rubbed those little melting ice cubes on it, flipping channels. I stretched out. I got past channel sixty when a pink leg filled the screen. There was stuffed nasal breathing. Then a girl's face with the hair drawn back too tight, her mouth ringed with lipstick and spit.

It was only a second before a body slid in and covered up the face. Then the camera circled around and found the girl again: she had a wide-open mouth and something was in it. You couldn't tell at first that it was a cock. It looked like an arm. Her eyes were shut, she was gagging. Our room was freezing. My mother hadn't shut off the air conditioning right. The girl was about to open her eyes but then the screen went black and a message came up: *Charge to Room? Press One to Continue.* I wanted to watch it. It was synchronicity.

My cheek was numb from the ice and I pressed one. The movie started up in another scene, though, as if it didn't pause in the right spot. I put two pillows behind my head. I stuffed one in between my thighs. Another girl was there now, a different girl who was blond and chubby, kneeling on a glass table. This girl was wearing a purple thong and see-through high heels. A penis banged her across her cheeks. She was laughing at that. My heart was going crazy. 'You like sucking me?' a guy's voice said. 'Yeah? You wanna suck me? Do you? Yeah?' Then, that second girl, her mouth red and wide, looked right at the camera. She was so different than that first girl who'd kept her eyes tightly closed. This girl was actually talking with that penis and trying to play with it to get it in her mouth, going, 'Yeah, gimme, yeah, gimme. I wanna suck you so bad. Gimme.'

'Look at her,' a guy's voice said. 'Look how much this slut wants it.'

I didn't feel the pillows behind me anymore. There was air in my chest where there was supposed to be beating. This wasn't like masturbation at all. I wasn't even touching myself. I was going to come without touching myself.

That girl's cheeks were so red, her eyes always stayed open, she was looking up at the guy and literally begging for it. *Gimme gimme gimme, please!* I realized, then, that her hands were tied behind her back. Her hands were tied and it popped in her mouth. She was laughing, she was so happy and tied. Her sucking was limbless, magnetic. I felt my head moving in time; I didn't have thoughts. Then all of a sudden the guy pulled out of her mouth and the cock was hot red, he was shaking it, squirting her lips with this cream. God, I'd never seen that before, all that stuff spraying out of him! The tied-up girl, she started going crazy, like groping around for it with her head like a baby bird, and his fingers were pushing the white stuff that landed on her face back into her mouth. She wanted that cock back in her too, she was groping and panting and I could barely watch her like that. Then another guy untied her and immediately she started rubbing herself, lying down spread on the glass table. Her wrists were all red and she still had drops on her face that looked like glue. She was rubbing herself furiously, she started pushing her thong inside herself and humping the air towards the camera.

'She loves it, she loves it, look at her go!'

My eyes were slit, I couldn't look straight at it, her pussy, her thong, how much she was rubbing herself and pushing that thong up inside of her and pulling it out and they showed that, in close-up, the most close-up I'd ever seen, her fingers rubbing and fabric going inside herself, everything was red and swollen and hospital-like.

My cheek started to hurt again. Then the first girl came back into the picture. She bent down and opened her fresh lipsticked mouth into the mouth of the second girl and they started kissing, there were guys around them, cocks pointed out at the top of the screen, and the first girl, she had something in her mouth, it was globby and creamy and she dripped it out of her lips slowly into the second girl's. They were moaning and passing that stuff between them, opened lips, like spit, white glue, and they were licking each other's tongues and lips and both of them were moaning together, one's eyes open, one's eyes shut. I felt so woozy and high that I shut my eyes and came; it felt painful and electric, like a shocking inside-out. Hot water gushed from me. I grunted. Fuck. I wet my side of the bed.

I couldn't find the TV converter. My legs ached. I needed a towel. The converter was on the floor. I didn't know how much that cost.

When my family came back, I was outside on the balcony waiting. The sun was as hot as it could be in the day. My mother came in last, behind my dad, then Jody and Jeff. No one was talking. My mother shut herself in the bathroom right away and didn't even look to see where I was. Jeff stared at me through the screen doors but he didn't say anything or smile. It was like he was fascinated by my new face. My cheek must've been glistening from the sun. Jody jumped on the bed, the dry side. 'Where's Myra?' she asked. Jeff pointed at the balcony. Jody looked like she felt sorry for me. Maybe they'd all made a pact or something. Don't talk to her until she talks to you.

Wind cried through the ribs of the palm leaves. My dad turned on the TV. It was going to be that channel! I opened the screen door to come in and stop it. The channels were flipping.

No one could fucking look at me anymore. Because I got pissed on and slapped, called my mom a bitch and watched porn, my whole family hated me now.

GAYL: Nice, nice. Pornography and shame.

LEE: Listen, come on, it wasn't her fault.

GAYL: Again with the fault. So whose fault was it?

LEE: It was Myra's instinct to apologize to her family to make everything better and, like, she didn't realize that *that* was the problem, not the piss, not the slap, not wanting to get fucked, not the porn. She wasn't coming back from this trip as herself. She wasn't coming back the same safe little person she left as. Her monstrous new face was a sign of that.

GAYL: Okay, fine. I'll accept that for now.

§

It was my last chance to get outside before the taxi came to take us to the airport. I had on a big straw hat and Jody's Sophia Loren glasses. My mom didn't try to stop me from leaving but she handed me her watch. Twenty minutes, she said without looking at me. We'd eat dinner at the airport. We had two flights to get home. The sun was still hours from going down. My cheek felt like matches were being struck and lit against it. But it occurred to me as I left the four of them packing that I was now free of my mother's desire for my life to be safe.

I walked to that woman's store in the alley, freaked out the whole time that I was going run into him. The bird woman sat on the same little stool outside, in the same pounds of turquoise. She stood up when I went in through the beaded curtains saying hi, but she didn't come in after me. The walls of the shop were cherry-coloured. Dark wood bookshelves with angels carved at the top were packed with trinkets and blankets. Mobiles of birds made of gold-painted paper hung all over the ceiling. Her shop smelled the same as his room. I was wearing big sunglasses and a hat but I knew she recognized me.

The woman didn't come inside the store for a while. There were these coral and beaded necklaces at the cash, pinned in a glass box like specimens. I just wanted that woman to tell me if that guy had a contagious disease. I knew her slap wouldn't cause all this swelling. I would not be able to go back to school looking like this.

'You want some help, sweetheart?' The woman was suddenly behind me.

I realized that people call each other names during sex to turn themselves on.

I knew the woman could see how ballooned and red my cheek was even though I was almost all covered up.

'Try this on,' the woman said. She opened up the door of the specimen box and held up a spiky necklace that had some turquoise in the collar part.

'No thanks,' I said.

Did I contract some kind of contagious disease from his piss?

The woman bent down below the glass box and rummaged around. She was rustling through tissue paper, stacked boxes. Then she held up a necklace with a plain leather strap. It had a tiny black pendant in a teardrop shape. It had red and green and yellow stripes.

'This is malachite,' she said.

Before I could think to say no or yes or whatever, she was putting it on me. She was touching my hair, lifting it up to fasten the clasp. It was really tight at my throat.

'This is a good one for young women,' she said. The black pendant felt like a bone. 'It's protection.'

The woman brought me over to a full-length mirror and I looked at myself with the necklace on. I wasn't looking so much at the necklace as I was looking at her trying to diagnose me. Jody was just like, 'You'll go see Dr. Bernhard at home. It'll get better.' My dad especially seemed unconcerned. 'No big deal,' he said, one-upping Jody. My mom got mad at him when he said that. 'Not to you,' she hissed.

'This necklace is a very powerful talisman against violence,' the woman said, fingering the teardrop, then laying it back down softly on my neck.

Why'd she think I needed a talisman against violence? I needed protection against disease from blowing into one of your fucking ocarinas!

'It's forty-five dollars. A special piece, handmade,' the woman said.

'I don't have any money on me.' I gave away my money to that fucking woman and him.

The woman sneaked behind the cash and set a prickly, long-limbed plant on the counter. 'You should put some of this on your cheek,' she said. 'It's very healing for whatever's going on under there.'

The woman tapped her chest, which was covered with turquoise. There was New Age music playing. I put my hand on the black bone necklace. The woman used an X-acto knife to cut off a piece of the plant. There was see-through cream dripping from where she cut. She squeezed some of it on her fingers and tried to touch my cheek. No fucking way, I pulled away. The woman held out the plant piece to me. It looked like a headless lizard, I thought. I took some of the oozing. It was cool. It felt all right.

'Three times a day,' the woman said. 'No more sun.'

'I'm leaving, anyway,' I said. *Bitch*.

'My name is Olinda.' She was smiling tightly. 'I'm going to give you a deal on the necklace.'

Olinda went behind the counter again. She put the lizard plant in a paper bag.

I took off my sunglasses and hat. I actually wanted this bitch's opinion: is getting slapped by a stranger what you mean by violence? I didn't know what the fuck a talisman was.

Olinda didn't look shocked that I had a huge swollen rash, a contagious disease. I wanted to ask her why she thought I needed protection. I knew that that was going to torment me at home. Jen wouldn't know, Jody wouldn't know, Dr. Bernhard wouldn't know either. No one would know why I needed protection.

'You can pay me by mail, if you'd like,' Olinda said.

All of a sudden I felt panic, because I really didn't want to see Elijah again, especially looking like this. Maybe he was going to walk right in, maybe pass by on his way to dinner with *her*. I put my hat and sunglasses back on. I don't know if Olinda knew I was freaking out. My cheek felt redder with that ooze from the plant. It was like I had shellac on top of fresh hives.

'I don't have any money,' I said. 'I have to go now. We're leaving in half an hour.'

'You can just send it. I trust you. You are ... ?'

'Myra.'

'Ahhh ... ' Olinda's face creased, connecting all of her features. *'I am Myra Breckinridge, whom no man will ever possess ... '*

I didn't know what she was talking about.

Olinda made me write down my address and email for her

on a brown paper bag. She stood too close. I felt the stink of incense. My cheek started to sting. Then she gave me one of her cards, slid her arm through mine and walked me to the hanging beads. I wondered how she ever locked her store at night because there was no door.

'You're a very sensitive person.' Olinda leaned into me like she was my age. Her lipstick was cracking. She was probably younger than my mother but she had way more wrinkles from being in the sun. She lifted the brim of my hat. Her lips touched my forehead.

'Key West is a darkly spiritual neighbourhood.' Her voice was tinny, like it could travel directly into my brain. 'A lot of souls, like your lover, have landed here.'

I felt tight. He is not my lover, I wanted to scream. He's a macho creep with a bleeding fucking girlfriend!

'I think you know what I mean.' Olinda's lips were still under the brim of my hat. 'You've got the look that attracts them.'

I dropped the paper bag that she gave me on purpose. I had to crouch down away from her to get it. What fucking look? What look did I have? I stood up a few feet backwards, outside. The alleyway walls were white and scribbled on.

'And you're innocent,' Olinda laughed. 'Not like these Spring Break sluts. So they like that even better.'

Fuck you fuck you fuck you, bitch! Do you even know what happened to me? That guy Elijah doesn't like me, he hates me. He didn't even want to have sex with me! He has a girlfriend and she slapped me so hard.

I ran out of Olinda's store with the brown paper bag, the headless plant. My cheek burned like it was peeling off. I didn't want to be innocent. I wanted to be a slut like those girls in that porno! I did. I swear. I wished I wished I wished I was a slut. God, why'd that woman slap my face? Why didn't he do anything?

I couldn't believe I had to go home like this, on a plane like this: the ugliest virgin in the world. I was going to have to see Jen and Charlene like this. Maybe this urge to lie to Jen, to be jealous of her, maybe she wasn't really my friend. Jen, Charlene, all of them. Maybe I shouldn't have any friends and maybe that'd be easier. Maybe I should just find some guy to fuck, someone who likes an ugly red cheek. I should wear see-through high heels and swap sperm with a girl.

At the airport Jody asked me where I'd gotten the necklace. I told her I'd found it in the sand but she didn't believe me.

'You know what those colours mean, right?'

'Of course I know,' I snapped. My father looked over, he heard my tone. Jeff had his head in my mother's lap. Both of my parents were headached and done.

'Rastafari,' Jody whispered. 'You don't know what a Rasta-farian is, do you?'

Jody touched my necklace and I could tell that she liked it. Some guy at school had given her a Bob Marley DVD. Jody said that Rastafarianism was a religion of peace and that it was kind of like Judaism, but from Jamaica. She said that Rastafarians worship Jah. 'It's like the name Eli-JAH, right? Or Hallelu-JAH. Get it? It's their word for God. It comes from Hebrew.'

My stomach felt twisted. Elijah, God. My mother didn't look like she'd been on vacation. Her face was pale, her mouth down-turned. I asked Jody if she knew what a talisman was.

'Magical protection against evil.' She knew, of course. 'It's an African thing. A talisman is something you have on you like a little arrowhead or something. It's supposed to break into pieces, like, if you're actually in danger.'

My mother got sick on the airplane, drinking coffee after coffee. Jody let me keep her sunglasses on the whole time.

I hoped this tight black Rastafarian necklace was a talisman against violence. Because now I felt monstrous and violent. I could not be mothered at all anymore.

✖✖

Make-Believe

*H*ello to the Angel I met on the beach. I have been thinking about Canada. I have never been to Canada. Send me a picture. I miss your sweet face.

My sweet face was still knobbed on one side like a toad's. The email came from that woman's store, Olinda@NewMoonTrad-ingMagick.com. I didn't write back because I wasn't sure what to say. The next message came for me six hours later.

The beautiful thing about you, Angel, is that you don't even know how beautiful you are. Don't ever take off the necklace I made for you.

He made me the necklace? It occurred to me that he was going to leave that woman to come up here to me. He was thinking about Canada. He made me the necklace. The talisman!

Okay tell me when you want to come, I wrote back. *Oh my god, thank you for the necklace!*

There was a knock at my door. I shut down the computer. It was both my parents together.

'Can't she open a window?' my father asked, moving in and swatting the air.

My mother flinched. 'Do it yourself.'

My father wrestled with my window until it unstuck. Then he bent down and huffed the cold air from the screen. It was overdramatic. My father's hair wasn't combed. His nose was still red from the sun in Key West.

'You looking forward to going back to school?' My mom's voice was too quiet. She sat down on the edge of my bed.

'You know I'm not.'

'You've been using the cortisone,' my dad said. 'So it's already getting better.'

'You can go out with Jen and Charlene and those girls, you know. You can sleep over at Jen's. We discussed that. That's fine with us now.'

There's this guy, this man who thinks I'm beautiful and he made me this necklace that protects me and he's going to come here and see me!

'We want you to be happy … ' My father's voice cracked.

I looked at him. He covered his face with both hands.

'It's okay, Myra. He's okay.'

I thought of a hyena, shot in the foot.

'I'm not okay, Irene! Don't put words in my mouth.'

I could only look at my mother. Not the force field of pain that was suddenly my father.

'You know when you have a fight with Jen, or one of your friends, Myra?' My mother's voice was too calm. 'Well, your dad and I have had a lot of fights lately … '

My dad rubbed his face hard. 'Why did we have to do this at the same time?'

Both of our faces were too red and sore, it felt weirdly genetic.

'You can leave now, Neil, if you want.'

'No!' my father screamed, his snout scrunched. 'You made me do this with you. Let's finish it. Christ. She's not a child anymore.'

I wished Jody were here in my room, Jeff too.

'Your father and I think that it would be better if we took a break from each other,' my mother said.

Then my father stumbled forward as if he were going to punch a wall.

'Just leave now, Neil,' my mother commanded.

My father changed directions and lurched out of my room.

'He's just upset,' my mother said. 'He'll be okay. He's an adult.'

I mean, I knew my parents didn't have a great relationship, I'd even told Jen before that I thought they should get a divorce like her parents. But now it felt like a hammer, a table cracked down the middle.

'I have a lot of interests, things I need to do, Myra ... '

'When's it going to happen?' My room gusted with cold.

'Oh, Myra ... '

'What?'

My mom leaned in towards me. I wrapped my blankets up to my chin.

'I'm sorry. You can't really understand right now, can you?'

I knew my mom had gotten married to my dad when she was nineteen, like all those girls on Spring Break. She was pretty much the same age as Jody was now. It almost didn't seem possible. I was hugging myself. My mother was sitting on the edge of my bed telling me that she was going to teach English in Korea for a year.

'A *year*? Korea? That's so far. Did you tell Jody?'

'She's okay with it,' my mom said. 'But are you?'

'You're going alone there?'

'No.'

'God, I knew it ... '

'Wait, Myra. My god, what do you think? I'm going with Sarah and Jon, the couple I met at my Spanish class this year.'

'I can't believe it, I mean we just went away! Jeff is only fourteen!'

'Myra, I know you can't understand this right now.'

I didn't know if my mother ever had a boyfriend before marrying my father. I didn't want to be so upset. I wanted her to get the fuck out of my room.

'Your cheek is going to clear up before school. Things are going to be fine if you keep using that cream.'

My mother hugged me heavily then, on top of my blankets. I couldn't untangle myself to hug her back or push her off. I couldn't believe she was leaving. We had to live alone with my dad?

'It's okay that you're mad at me, Myra,' my mother whispered into my hair. 'I might be mad too, if I were you.'

'You don't know what's going on with me,' I croaked.

'It would make me feel a lot steadier right now, Myra, if you could just try to understand things from my perspective.'

My mother was always so young-looking that strangers thought me and Jody and her were all sisters. I held on to my necklace and closed my eyes. Elijah made me this necklace, this chain that was locked on me now. He said it was beautiful that I didn't know how beautiful I was.

GAYL: She's forgetting things! Tripping. Like what about me?
LEE: No, no, she's managing all right.
GAYL: Man, I just want to get to the dirty stuff now.
LEE: Leave her alone, she's lonely. Let's leave her alone.

§

My red shiny miniskirt, white leather booties and cut-off white V-neck T to distract from my face. I was supposed to meet Jen at her place with Charlene. I was supposed to show off my tan lines and trade stories about March Break. But at my mother's makeup table with the daytime light setting, I thought my cheek looked medieval or something: I was a leprous species close-up. I shoved my hand down my skirt. Thank god I could make myself come. That was the only thing I could be thankful for. I could come in seconds now just by squeezing my legs together, squeezing inside. My mom had at least fifty different tubs inside her table. I dipped into two of the peach-coloured foundations and rubbed my entire face with the stuff. Then I turned the light setting to night and blue-purple dots bounced off my fresh mask. It didn't look bad, it looked kind of glamorous, actually. I painted on another layer of the stuff, then I dusted with powder, smoothing over the cracks. The lights on my skin were like cars on the road.

'You look hot, My!' Jen came bounding down the stairs of her place. She hugged me and kissed me on both cheeks. At least my cheek didn't hurt as much anymore. 'You look like an actress or something!' She smelled like coconut cream. Jen said once, drunk, that she thought I had a good body. I knew by the way she checked me out, without wanting to be too obvious, that she had that thought again. She was always tabulating thoughts and weighing them out. I was thinking I should give her a compliment too. Jen was tanned to the point of near-burn. She always wore the right amount of makeup because her dad's girlfriend was a clerk at Holt Renfrew and she'd taught her how to do it right. All the guys liked Jen. She'd had three boyfriends already, all in Grade 12. I followed her up the stairs to her bedroom. There was a flask on her pillow. She gave me a swig.

'Our trip was fucking awesome. My, you have to tell me all about yours when Char comes. Tell us all the dirty details. Oh god, Dave and my mom were totally relaxed in Cabo and we tried to get the Mexican guys at our hotel to sneak booze into my drink. This guy, the bartender, did stuff like that, he said, for *caliente* girls like me. He was nineteen and Dave knew I was hot for him and he almost tried to set us up. He kept making jokes at dinner saying, You know this girl is going to be at the pool later, right? His name was Ricky, but I called him his real name, Ricardo, he was so fucking embarrassed that Dave was doing that. It was cute though, really. I've got his email, we're gonna talk.'

Jen smiled. She took three long chugs off the flask. She was already planning our graduation trip. I was thinking about how I was going to tell Jen about Elijah. Charlene was black and I wondered if she'd think it was weird that I was with a black guy who I met on the beach. Who wanted me to touch his cock. Who pissed on me. Who was going to come here. Jen would fucking freak out if she knew.

'That's cool about Ricardo,' I said.

'Yeah, yeah, he's amazing. A rock star. You'd think so too. Next time your parents should let you come with me to Cabo. We'll have a fucking blast! We're old enough in Mexico to really drink. Tequila, baby. The good stuff.'

I don't think my mother ever liked Jen. My mother had looked tiny with her backpack on, standing at the door to say goodbye. She looked like one of those Korean women on her book cover, dressed up and silent and stiff, against a wall of rock.

'I'm gonna keep in touch with Ricardo, maybe he has a hot friend for you too.'

I knew at that moment in Jen's room that I wouldn't ever be with a guy like she was with a guy. It all seemed too obvious, too ordinary. I liked men who were older than me. I liked black men. I liked musicians. This was the kind of guy I wanted to be with. This was the kind of person I wanted to understand. I didn't want to understand Jen or her tallied-up, shallow conquests.

'Myra, is something wrong? You seem kind of sad or something, girlfriend.'

'Nah, I'm okay. I just want more to drink.'

I hated my mother and father. I was bored with Jen. I wanted to watch porn. I'd found this website for free, it was a service or something that delivered these video clips to your inbox. They were a minute, sometimes more, of these girls getting fucked, like what I saw in Key West but even more extreme, with headings like: *asschick, teenwhore, slutgettingcock.* Jeff had bawled at the door when the taxi arrived for my mom. Jody gave my mom a massive hug. My father hid out in the basement alone. I let my mom kiss my forehead. Her lips were lukewarm. I watched her struggle into the taxi, that backpack was half of her height. I got a new porno teaser delivered every day.

'My parents are getting a divorce,' I said to Jen. I was hiccupping. It occurred to me that my mother had planned her escape.

'Seriously, Myra? Oh god, I'm so sorry.' Jen passed me the flask.

Those video clips made me really feel fucking. A cock going in and in and in. Girls' mouths gagging and jacking wide.

'Actually, I'm not sorry, Myra. Welcome to the club!'

Charlene was ringing the bell. Jen kissed me on the lips before she ran for the door. One long swig and I finished the flask. Elijah was coming here. My mother was gone. I wore all this makeup and saw all this porn. Me: on the edge of being free.

§

In the blue smoked-up backyard with Jen and Charlene, I ended up drinking five big plastic cups from the keg. I started crying, pretty uncontrolled, when Jen told me that my face looked orange.

'You should let my dad's girlfriend give you a lesson, My, it's okay, it's just too much powder, Ella's so good, I swear, I use everything she taught me.'

Jen was right up in my face and I shoved her away with both hands.

'I'm just trying to help you, Myra!' Jen screamed.

I had to stop crying.

'Oh god, I care about you!' Jen moaned way too loud. 'Your face looks weird, My, seriously, why'd you put all that crap on your face! I know what you're going through, you don't think that I know?'

'Leave me alone, you fucking butch!' I meant to say *bitch* and Charlene laughed that I said *butch*.

Charlene slung her arm around Jen's shoulder, coaxing her away from me. Obviously Charlene thought I was totally disgusting. I stopped crying and smeared my face. Charlene and Jen looked like two sheep nuzzling each other. They moved towards the weeping willow at the end of the yard where a group of girls smoked. I watched Jen get swallowed up in the female herd. It was totally pathetic.

I stood at the side fence of the backyard connecting the groups of people into dots. Leaves from a tree in the yard next door scratched the top of my head. No one came and talked to me. After a while, I went back inside the house. There was a staircase at the back of the kitchen. I walked through where a couple of kids I didn't know were smoking at a table. One of the girls stared at me as I passed her. I hadn't seen her before at our school. She had frizzy brown hair, a long nose and she was strange in the eyes. They were brown but they had this bluish glow to them. She seemed calf-eyed, the colours streaking, as if the calf were being electrocuted.

'That was me!' Lee said later, proud. 'I was backlit, watery, electroshocked.'

'I didn't know if you noticed me in the kitchen there, or if I was just noticing you.'

'Of course I saw you, Myra. You were alien-like.'

'God, yeah, you're right. I was skimming the floor!'

'Slimy, sucky and isolated.'

'The Electrocuted and the Alienated ... '

There was bubbling in my stomach. I felt sick from all the beer. The group at the table laughed as I walked up the back stairs. I didn't know if they were laughing at me. The guy whose party it was, I knew he had an older brother. The older brother was the one who got us the keg. Jody once told me that stairs off a kitchen were for a maid because a maid was not supposed to be seen. This was when Faith worked for us, every single week. I remember Jody was pissed off because she'd asked my mother to not let Faith go in her room. Jeff was listening to us argue, pretending to read.

'She's a maid,' I said to Jody. 'She's paid to clean and your room's a mess.'

'My room is my private property, thank you very much. And Faith is not a maid.'

'Of course she's a maid!'

'No,' Jody said. 'She just helps mom with the housework. She's a cleaning lady. I mean, a cleaning woman. A domestic worker. She comes once a week, not every day. She doesn't look after us.'

'Yeah, but how is a cleaning lady different than a maid?'

'A cleaning woman is a domestic worker who works in lots of people's homes. She's freelance. She can raise her fees. She doesn't need to walk the dog, for example. She doesn't need to put kids to bed. And my room is fucking private. End of story.'

'Well, if you don't want Faith in your room then we should clean the toilets, we should vacuum, we shouldn't have her in our house at all. That'd be better, anyway.'

Jody got mad at me. 'Mom is giving Faith a job, Myra. You don't know all the details. It's complicated.'

I rolled my eyes. 'I know she was abused, all right?'

Jeff put down his book and we watched Jody storm out. 'Mom is *sponsoring* Faith, Myra. That costs a lot of money. You don't know everything, you know.'

I was totally parched climbing up the maid's stairs. The floor felt like paste. Faith never came back from Jamaica. On the slanted third floor there was a tiny landing with two doors to enter. I faced the brown one that was open a bit and plastered with skateboarding stickers. Elijah was fifteen years older than everyone here. Faith returned to a husband who abused her, she had to live there on an island with him forever.

I saw the older brother in his room. He lay on a mattress on his side on the floor, reading a book without a cover. His hair was greasy, sticking up, with one gluey black curl on his forehead. An old fried egg on a plate on the floor was orange and hard. I entered and the older brother looked up at me. It didn't look like he was surprised to see me – a freak with peach-coloured makeup half-off. The older brother was drinking a plastic red cup of beer. His mattress had faded flowers on the sheets.

I was glad to be away from Jen and Charlene. The older brother looked smart. Most girls are fucking mean. If they're nice, it's an act.

The older brother motioned for me to come over, come closer, as if he knew that I was having these bitch-like thoughts. I stumbled and sat on his mattress.

'I drank too much,' I whispered. My white T-shirt felt wet. I didn't know if I'd drooled or spilled beer. 'I walked up the maid's stairs … '

The older brother's eyes roamed around my face. I smelled the oil of his hair.

'We used to have a domestic worker named Faith but you guys have real stairs for a real maid.'

(GAYL: Oh shit. Don't let her get into this topic. Forward, forward. She's with a guy!)

'I was talking to you when you came up the stairs,' the older brother said.

I remembered that the older brother wasn't even in the room when I got to the top of the stairs, I didn't think.

'I wanted to trick whoever was coming up the stairs, like, trust in them and trust in myself … '

The older brother assumed that I understood, the way he was looking at me nodding, trying to get me to nod too.

'See, I'm experimenting with two complicated actions, to see if I can do them both at once. I mean read and intuit. Like, read and feel someone's need for connection intertwined with my own need for connection. See how we can play these little games with ourselves?'

All of a sudden, the older brother hugged me. It felt so strange that I went blank. He smashed me into his chest, his oil-smelled shirt. I didn't have enough air with my lips on his chest. My secrets weren't going to be secrets anymore. I pushed myself out of the older brother's arms.

'You know, you're different from the rest of those girls down-stairs,' he said. The older brother stared at my face. 'You're way more mature.'

Yeah, I almost had sex with a guy who pissed on me!

'You don't have to be weirded out or anything, okay?'

'Okay.'

'You know I'm Aaron, right? I'm Jeremy's bro.'

Aaron patted the space right beside him on his bed, like – come a bit closer, not gonna bite you. I nodded and nodded. It was easy to do. I lay down then and Aaron lay down beside me. I dissolved into the mattress, down through the floor.

Aaron kissed my forehead. 'You smell good,' he said. 'Like rosehip rustic rummy delight.'

Then he started kissing down my nose, then over my top lip. All of a sudden he was on my mouth and we were kissing. I felt his tongue in my mouth. I smelled our beer. We did that for a while until I shifted away.

'I don't know,' I said. I felt weird all of a sudden.

'It's cool, it's cool. You're amazing. Whatever.'

I closed my eyes and Aaron started reading out loud. I focused on his hands. The knuckles were purple and over-cracked.

'"Love is a sign of our wretchedness,"' Aaron read. '"God can only love himself. We can only love something else."'

'Uhm-hum,' I said, in the middle of a wave. I suddenly felt too drunk all over again. I'd screamed at Jen downstairs, fucked up our entire relationship, and I'd just made out with Aaron for no reason.

(LEE: Yo yo yo! Don't forget about me. You saw me. We communed.)

I covered my mouth so that nothing would come out. Aaron looked at me funny. I had to go to sleep.

'I know I just met you,' Aaron whispered. My eyes tried to keep open. 'But there's this space in me, I hope it's not too wretched to say it … Uh, there's this space in me, kind of opening up … Like, I think that space is opening up in me to love you.'

I grunted.

'It's okay,' Aaron said. He turned me on my side, off my back. 'This will be your position tonight.'

Aaron was being so nice to me. But I didn't feel a thing falling into his bed. I wanted to make out with Elijah. Elijah naked, a god. God can only love himself. I can only love something else.

'Myra? Are you okay? Your cheek is kind of bleeding or something. Wake up for a sec.'

I'd left a note for my father saying that I was sleeping at Jen's but I'd already spent my cab fare contributing to the keg. Now I was trying to remember the minutes before I got drunk. Pissing, falling around in the bathroom at Jen's while Jen and Charlene were putting on rouge. The flask had been filled up again and was drained. We three in a cab. Me on Jen's lap. The driver's bad eyes. I was going to vomit.

Aaron stroked something damp on my forehead, then he dabbed into my cheek. It felt freaky, like my head had no neck.

'It's okay now, it's okay. You don't have to wake up.'

I must've passed out. There was smoke and rose smell. Aaron had a bathroom right off his bedroom. Shadows were coming in and out. I could see them through my eyelids.

'I like this strain,' a girl said. That was her from downstairs, I knew.

'You're not going to test it all tonight, are you, dudes?' Aaron laughed.

'We've got lots to bag up,' a guy said. 'The party next week.'

'For King Anarchist.' Again, that was her. The blue-lit calf from downstairs.

The smoke was perfumed.

'What's up with that chick with the Rasta necklace?' the girl said.

'She's an angel,' someone said.

An angel? God, no. I couldn't open my eyes. If I opened my eyes they'd spill over like eggs.

'Her face is bleeding.'

'She's fine, Lee. All good.' Aaron's fingers touched my forehead. It was soaked. All I wanted was to open my eyes. All I wanted was to vomit my thoughts.

'She doesn't look so hot, I mean I think … '

There was a violent push up and I felt myself gag. My eyes still didn't open but I could see pearly white. All over my chin there was hair and hot fizz.

I heard Aaron shout: 'Get a towel, man, fuck!'

The girl held a plastic bag up at my mouth that was filled to the top with papers and food. I didn't know if she thought I was stupid for puking. I had one hand on my cheek. It's true that it was bleeding.

The girl handed me a towel to put under my head. She wiped some blood off my cheek with her hand.

'You okay now?' she asked. She wiped her hand on her jeans.

I looked at her. I tried to say yes. The girl looked pissed. She held the full plastic bag of my puke and walked out of the room with it.

LEE: I had to leave you there with Aaron, even though it wasn't my instinct to.

GAYL: It's good that you were gonna be her friend. Because there's no way I was gonna protect her.

LEE: Yeah, yeah. I think that's already apparent.

§

'Myra? This is Myra?'

There was a patch of static on the line. It was only six in the morning. I thought it was him.

'Myra, right?' the voice said to someone else. 'Myra. Hello? Hello?'

I pressed the phone to my ear to hear through the noise. I wanted it to be him. 'Yeah, it's me.'

There was another long line of static. I thought this is what it would sound like when my mother called from Korea.

'Who is this?' I asked. I heard coughing, a laugh.

'Your friend entered you in a contest,' the voice said. It was deep like his, but it didn't have an accent. 'We picked your name for the grand-prize win but I have to ask you a few questions first.'

My room was still dark. It wasn't Elijah. It occurred to me that Jen had written my name on some raffle ticket or something from Holt Renfrew. Or maybe this was her idea of a really mean fucking joke. Me and Jen hadn't spoken since the party. The first day back at school her and Charlene totally ignored me.

'Are you a senior or a freshman?'

'I'm in Grade 10,' I said. What the fuck's a fresh man?

'Name of your school?'

'Mount Pleasant Secondary.'

'What's your height, weight and date of birth?

'Um ... Five-two. November twenty-third. One hundred and seven. Why?'

When I went to Dr. Bernhard for the second time about my cheek because of the bleeding, he did a full physical on me. He said that what was going on was a manifestation of acne, that girls my age have a throng of active hormones. Jody had some acne when she was my age. Before she went back to residence, she told me to put toothpaste on my cheek.

Dr. Bernhard asked me if I had a boyfriend. Then: did I know about safe sex? I remembered the thawing flesh of hot dog with Jen. I told Bernhard I knew.

'Hair colour, eye colour.'

'Brown. Brown.'

'Hair down below?'

I felt the receiver on my mouth. I heard my heart beat in my throat.

'You have hair on your vagina, don't you?'

Jen had hair. Charlene had hair.

'It's brown?'

The voice knew. Static was constant, electric.

'And when did you first start menstruating, Myra?'

I was flinching inside. Dr. Bernhard said that girls had to know about avoiding pregnancy. He said that we would do an internal only if I was not a virgin.

'Eleven,' I said.

'Oooh, baby. That's early.'

It *was* Elijah. I heard his accent. He was trying to hide it.

'You got breasts that early as well, little girl?'

My breath was going unnaturally fast. I had to tell Dr. Bernhard that I was a virgin. If I could have lied I would have lied. I would have washed my virginity away in a flood.

'What size brassiere do you wear?'

I heard laughing in the background.

'34C.'

'You're not still a virgin, are you?' His voice got clearer through the buzzing. 'Yeah, you're not a virgin. She's not a virgin. I told you. That's hot as fuck.'

He was talking to me and to someone else. I remembered that woman's slap. I was going to hang up.

'What did it feel like to have a cock inside you?'

The phone was a weapon.

'Come on, did it hurt the first time?'

My kneecaps were touching. I wanted to scream.

'Yeah, it hurt a lot,' I said.

A bat-screech laugh came from somewhere behind him.

'She's lying,' I heard.

'Nah, she's not lying. She's finally fucked a boy.'

I was going to hang up. I was going to hang up.

'So you're not a frigid little bitch anymore?'

I threw the phone down on the floor hard enough to break. I cupped my hand between my legs.

Telling myself not to be scared didn't work.

GAYL: Oh boy. Oh yeah. She likes the sexual attention.

LEE: Attention? Are you crazy? That's not attention – that's harassment!

GAYL: Listen to what you're saying about *sexual charge*. That it's nothing but harassment, are you for real?

LEE: Don't put your twisted contradictory banter onto me.

GAYL: Fine. Think what you want.
LEE: I think it's bullshit.
GAYL: I think it's kinky that she's scared.

§

Aaron raced through the yellow lights for no reason. He had a white Dodge Ram with plaid blankets on the seats. 'Love doobing and driving, oh yeah!' Aaron wasn't afraid of cops or getting busted. He knew the drug laws of the province code by code. He was in the process of becoming a member of the Marijuana Party and he'd been a grow apprentice last summer in B.C.

I was totally skipping school. My mother wasn't around to get a call from the VP. We hadn't even heard from her yet. My dad had never in his life spoken to one of my teachers before, so I thought, correctly, that there'd be space there for me to skip. Aaron said he'd lend me books for some 'real' high school education. We were going, first, he said, to deal with the 'money issue.' Aaron passed me the joint. The car was steady and fast.

This was the third time in my life I'd ever smoked pot. The first two times were with Jen who'd gotten it from her mom's boyfriend. I don't think I had completely inhaled with her, but even so, we got into hysterics about her cat licking itself with its head all contorted. It was cleaning between its legs in a field of black fur. We couldn't speak we were laughing so hard, saying imagine if we had to bend down inside ourselves to clean ourselves there, to clean our pussies like pussies?

'Pass it back, My. It's fucking strong shit. Chris is gonna love this strain.'

We were on our way to the old Molson Plant, where Aaron bought his stash together with Wils, who was in the room with Lee when she held the garbage can for my puke. Apparently they were all middlemen for Chris, who linked up to the market in the States. Lee called Chris the Anarchist King. Whatever that meant. I had a lot to learn. Aaron was right, high school was not the only place.

Lee was with Wils at the Plant when we arrived. I was terribly stoned. I'd put my mother's makeup back on my cheek even though the toothpaste had kind of helped dry it all out.

'I'm Lee,' Lee said.

'I know,' I said.

Lee was wearing a red fuzzy sweater. Her cheeks had tiny brown beauty marks high on the bone. Wils was a lot taller than Lee. He had a bowl cut and rectangular glasses. Lee and Wils looked like friends more than a couple.

We all smoked another J together. I was going at it without any thought of how fucked-up I'd be. Twenty-foot concrete vats were being used to grow plants.

'Chris says in Vermont they're not as discerning.'

'Whatever, this shit is stinky, dude.'

'He'll love it,' Lee said.

Aaron and Wils were like businessmen. So was Lee, she seemed at least twenty years old. Aaron took out a briefcase, or a satchel, made of black leather and a strap. Leather and a strap. I started to laugh. A video had been emailed to me that morning with a leather strap gag cutting into a girl's lips. She was sniffing this little white glob on the carpet and her tongue came out from around the gag, she was about to lap it up, when some guy off-screen above her started pulling on the gag, it was just like a leash, he kept pulling her head up by the gag. She looked like a dog, a pink-tongued and thirsty and excited little dog. *Gagged-cumeatingslut* was her name.

'I think I'm ready,' I said for some reason, forgetting exactly what my problems were.

Wils was beside me. His eyes were buggy and happy and glinted green. I think I was good but just really dizzy. Lee looked at me not sideways but diagonally. We were the same height. I felt something activate between us, like a wobbly plastic strip in the air. Aaron and Wils were talking about passages too, the pathways of drugs through Vermont to Miami. Lee kept looking at me on that angle, like trying to re-ignite and make real the thing that was wavering between us. The plants breathed. That's how stoned I could be. There was something between me and Lee, between me and the plants. The ceilings were vaulted. There was a growth between my legs: a pig's tail, corkscrewing pink. I needed to jam it into something. I needed to rub it against another pig. Maybe I'd never felt truly horny, just the preparation. Maybe this feeling, this tail, was its ultimate expression.

'Hey, Myra, wanna come to the bathroom with me?' Lee asked.

My tail receded. Aaron looked at me weirdly. He was measuring baggies with Wils off a huge bush ball of weed. The satchel was open, a calculator and a thermos inside.

'Are you guys done soon?' I asked.

Lee smiled at me. 'Just come,' she said

Lee held out her hand and I didn't take it, but I followed. We walked through the concrete hallway. Vents blew chemical air. Oil spotted the ground in zigzags.

The bathroom was small. Water dripped from the four-legged sink.

'You and Aaron are hot and heavy, huh?' Lee took the elastic out of her hair and shook it out.

'No, not a lot.'

'What do you mean not a lot?'

'I don't know. I mean not so much. We just met or whatever. You and Wils are together too?'

'Eighteen months,' Lee said. She looked at me behind her through the mirror. I slid down the wall to sit on the cold floor.

'Really?'

'Yeah. Why?'

'I don't know, I don't really see you two together.'

'Why not? That's bold. You don't even know me.'

Lee turned around and looked down at me. Her hair stood out from her skull like soft brown and black twigs.

'I don't know. Forget it.'

'No, what do you see? I want to know.'

My jaw was all stiff. 'You seem kind of off to the left of him. Bigger maybe, I don't know.'

'You see that?'

'Yeah, I guess.'

Lee watched me and pulled her hair back into a bun. 'Well, he's kind of a man-boy. But I like that.' Lee took out her stash wrapped in foil from her back pocket. 'What do you want to do tonight?'

'Smoke more,' I said.

'Okay, cool.'

Lee rolled a J on the medical-looking sink. 'Let's smoke all night and talk to the gods,' she said.

'We have to find them first.'

'Right. Invite them in.'

'Make them happy,' I said.

'Yeah. On our knees!'

I knew Lee knew what it was like to be on her knees, sucking a guy. I didn't know yet, but I pretended I did.

'Let's go back and tell our men,' Lee said. The joint was already lit. She was grabbing my arm to pull me up.

I forgot that we were talking about them. When Lee said *men*, I thought of Elijah. I thought of being on my knees for him. Elijah on my knees, on the phone, on his way. He told me that he was coming to Canada. I heard that bat-screeching laugh. Female.

'I don't want to go back yet,' I said. 'I can't.'

'Okay. You're right. You're okay. Let's stay a little longer.'

Lee sat down with me on the floor. I was trying to de-stone myself, to stop being scared. Lee took a drag off the joint, then she ground it out on the floor, watching me. I was shaking. Shaking like after an orgasm. I couldn't stop myself.

'You're okay,' Lee said. She put her hand on my shoulder.

'Okay, I know. I'm okay. But, uh, it's like … '

'What?'

'Uh … There's this guy who's supposed to come in from out of town to see me and I don't know what to do.'

'You mean the American guy?'

'How do you know?'

'You told me about him.'

'I did?'

'You said you were seeing some American guy and that he was imposing.'

'I did? I don't think I said that.'

'Yeah, you did. That first night we met. When you were puking. Right after you puked. You were talking about some American guy, that he was a musician, a lot older. You said you were seeing this guy and you missed him a lot.'

'I did?'

'Yeah. And you said he made you that necklace.'

'Oh god. Did everyone hear me?'

'No, they were smoking. They didn't care. You were just telling me.'

'What else did I say?'

'So is this guy a Rasta or what?'

My teardrop black-red-yellow-and-green talisman against violence.

'No. I mean, I don't think he is. I don't know. I really don't know. He's from Tanzania. God, I feel sick.'

'From telling me? From what?'

'No. I just feel really sick. I don't know how to deal with it, like, that he's coming here.'

'Well, he sounds cool, I guess. The Rasta from Tanzania.'

'No!'

'Why?'

It hit me then, everything that happened in Key West. I had not told anyone. There was just my scabbed-up cheek and my porn.

'What's the matter, Myra? You can tell me.'

I had to speak or I was going to faint.

'Okay, okay, okay ... I've got this picture in my head of him and, uh ... Okay ... It's going over and over, it's filling up my head, I can't stop it.'

'What's the picture?'

I held on to a metal leg of the sink.

'It's his body ... '

'What about his body? It's okay – just say it.'

'His body is so amazing. It smells like caramel.'

'What did you guys do together?'

'No, I mean. We didn't do ... No, I mean, fuck, I can't say it.'

'Say it, Myra. Just talk.'

'It's my hair, he's grabbing my hair and he's got it pulled back too tight and he's naked and my mouth is messed up with lipstick and spit and his cock's right there ... '

'Yeah?'

'And it's in front of my face and I'm dumb and I'm mute and he's calling me a bitch. Then he forces me to suck him or whatever, and when he takes himself out he sprays all over my face.'

Lee looked at me. I felt better and worse.

'You're not dumb,' she said, poking my shoulder.

I had no idea what she was thinking. We didn't know each other at all. I didn't even know what high school she'd gone to.

'It's okay that you see that,' Lee said slowly. 'I mean, there's nothing wrong with that.'

'Are you serious?'

'Well, I mean, what do you think that fucking is about?'

I felt relieved at first, that Lee was experienced. That she knew about fucking, that maybe she'd even watched porn like me, porn criss-crossing in my head every time I thought about Elijah: girls on glass tables, glue-shooting cocks, cunts in close-up.

Lee stood up. 'Myra, I asked what you thought fucking was about.'

'I don't know what fucking is about.'

'Well, I know. You mind if I say it?'

'No. Say it.'

Lee pulled me up off the floor. We were standing face to face.

'Fucking is dirty. You want to not have it all romantic and drippy. It's okay that you want it dirty with this guy. It's okay that you want that picture in your head to be true.'

Lee got quiet. I blushed. Heat shot through my thighs. What I thought was shame, she was saying, was not shame at all.

GAYL: True. Our bitch wants her backward-ass dreams to come true. Me and the man can make these kinds of dreams true.

§

There he was, shivering in a white robe. Elijah stood on the street across from my school, scanning the tops of the kids' heads for me.

The wind blew through him. He wasn't dressed right: head to toe pale and billowing in a thin-looking robe, dreadlocks up in a turban that looked like soft ice cream. He shifted from one foot to the other, searching me out. He was not half-naked and glistening like he was in Key West. I felt my heart pound. I could not cross the street.

I saw Jen and Charlene coming up arm-in-arm through the bodies of kids from our school. I took off my knapsack, dropped it on the ground pretending I needed something in there. I didn't know if Elijah had seen me yet. But I could feel Jen's body, her smell when she got close. She wore some fancy Holt Renfrew perfume.

'Look at that crazy guy,' I heard Charlene say to Jen. 'Look. Across the street.'

Jen and Charlene stopped about three feet away from me. I dug deeper in my bag. I found an old pear. Jen dropped her bag on the ground too. It was like she was copying me or something. Fuck.

'Weird,' Charlene said loudly. 'He's looking at us.'

I don't know why, but it felt like for a second that Jen was going to apologize to me. I imagined us being friends again, everything going back to normal. I took a bite of the mushy pear.

Then Jen said, 'No, he's not looking at us. He's looking at *Myra*.'

It was mean, how she said my name. She said *Myra* like she hated me. I stood up quickly and put my knapsack back on. I started to walk fast towards the school and I stepped on her bag by accident.

'Fuck!' Jen said. 'What the hell is wrong with you?'

'Sorry,' I muttered.

I felt Elijah from the other side of the street, his hands in the air like a vapour, an angel. My body started to shake. I held the bad pear. I was completely see-through.

'*Sorry*,' Jen mocked me in a squeaky voice.

'Don't be so fucking immature,' I said. I lurched past them, in the direction of school.

'Oh, don't be a fucking cunt!' Charlene said after me.

I stopped and turned around, in shakes. 'I *am* a cunt!' I yelled. They were both crouched down like frogs. I felt the pear skin split at a bruise. 'And you're both cunts too!'

I took a look across the street. Elijah walked out, in the middle of traffic, holding his arms out to stop the cars. The wind billowed his robe. He was all happy teeth. I smiled too. Charlene and Jen had out their phones.

Elijah had a beard growing of longish black moss. Cars beeped. He looked totally religious. It was weird he wasn't wearing a coat. I thought for a second of running, going to the principal. I could've even called my dad, who I knew was at home in the basement doing nothing. Jen and Charlene were watching me.

'He fucking *knows* her?' I heard Jen asking.

Elijah grabbed me tight by the wrist.

And I realized that *I* had made this happen. My thoughts had made this happen.

'Hi,' I breathed. His hand was a half-rough, half-smooth piece of ice.

'What happened to you?' Elijah peered at my cheek.

The scabs had not completely disappeared but I hid them under my mother's cream. I yanked my wrist away from him.

'I'm just hungry,' I said. I took another bite of the pear.

Elijah leaned in close to me, he got right up close. 'What happened to you, Angel? You don't need that crap on your face.'

He reached his finger out and swiped my cheek. Orange stuff came off.

'I'm not an angel!'

I knew that Jen and Charlene were fucking shocked to death that I was talking to this guy, that I knew this guy. This man was here from Key West for *me*.

'Okay, girl, okay, okay. So what are you hiding under there?'

There was mush in my mouth so I just shook my head. I felt the teardrop necklace heavy on my chest.

'I'm not hiding anything, okay?' I looked around. Charlene and Jen motioned to me to come over to them. 'I'm just on my way home.'

Elijah held out a business card. 'This is where I'm staying.'

I reached for the card but he pulled it away.

'You want it?'

'Yeah.'

'Come closer.'

'Nn-nnn.'

Jen and Charlene were watching, they were watching this. Scared.

Elijah put the card into a fold in his tunic. I licked my lips.

'Come and get it. It's in here.'

My heart freaked. I heard Charlene on the phone. I couldn't understand what she was saying, she was talking too fast.

'Those girls are jealous of you,' Elijah said. His lips brushed the top of my head.

Jen and Charlene would never know someone like Elijah. I, alone, knew this man. I was a different person than I'd been before Key West. I was starting to be friends with a girl older than me. I was living with my brother and my dad. I was making out all the time with Aaron who said he worshipped me. My mom left town two weeks ago and I hadn't heard from her yet. I was a different person from who I'd been before. Fuck Jen and fuck Charlene. I, alone, knew Elijah. This man had crossed the continent for me.

'Show those two girls over there that you know what to do,' Elijah whispered into my hair. 'Show them that I know all about you.'

I put my hand on Elijah's shoulder and Elijah slid my hand down to his waist.

Take that, frog cunts. This is my man.

Elijah slipped my free hand into the fold of his tunic. I felt him hard in there, moving around. He was forcing me to feel the length of his cock. I'd seen so many cocks now in my porn. Elijah's was big. I was as big as the sky. My body covered the jerking of what we were doing. I knew Jen and Charlene didn't know what to do. I knew what to do. I rooted around for the card from Elijah's hotel, his cock in my hand, squeezing when he pushed up. I had to bend down a little and lean into him more. I heard Elijah grunt. He was looking over my head at Jen and Charlene. He was making me go faster, squeeze harder all along his length. It was hurting my wrist and I was trying to get away. I'd do it later, I'd do it in his hotel. I'd do it on my hands and knees and look up at him just like those girls in the porns.

'Come on, girl, just do it. Finish up.'

'I can't,' I whispered.

I heard Jen say: 'Let's get a teacher.'

Charlene: 'The police.'

'Something's wrong with you, Angel, why're you so tight?'

'I'm not, I'm not tight.'

'You're tight, you're too tight.'

'I am not! I'm not tight!'

Jen and Charlene sped by us like flies. I smelled the rotten perfume.

'I'm not tight,' I whispered. 'My *pussy* is tight.'

Elijah snorted. I felt a stain of hot wet on his front. I whipped my hand out of his tunic holding the card. I had his number. I looked for Jen and Charlene but they were nowhere around.

'Where'd you learn to talk like that?'

My heart was beating too fast.

'You make me crazy, you know that?'

I wished I could've walked home with Jen and Charlene.

'I wanted you from three thousand miles away.'

A police car suddenly burned and screamed by. My breasts went hard inside my bra.

'But don't wear that crap on your face when you come see me. You're a sexier little bitch without that.'

The necklace he made me hit against a weird pulse.

'When should I come?'

'Tomorrow. Saturday. Day of action.' Elijah smiled. His jaw was like a sculpture. His white turban stood. 'You come and I'll fuck your tight pussy all night.'

Blood pounded so hard through my body, pumping and crooked like wires of light. I was going to scream his name when I was coming. I wanted my hands tied behind my back. Just like those sucked and slapped girls in my video clips. They always had to look the men in the eyes when they were coming. The guys wanted to see how much they were destroying them with their big hard cocks like hammers and pipes. It was amazing, that look in the girls' eyes, rabid eyes, glossy, pleading, unnameable eyes, like they loved being tortured and pounded and kept.

'You'll be there, yeah?'

'Yeah.'

I was breathless. Elijah walked away. I held my virginity up in my fist.

GAYL: *Shit.* I got nothing here. I've got nothing to say.

§

'I think you were actually degraded by this guy,' Lee said to me in the ravine near my house. A greenish light full of flies lit us up. I'd told her the whole Key West story, minus the part about the slap. 'And it's like you're still operating within a pattern of systemic degradation.'

'Systemic degradation? Degradation, you mean, because he pissed on me?'

'On your head. Uh, yeah. Where your brain resides. My other point being that you and Aaron don't do stuff like that, so why'd you do it with that guy?'

'How do you know me and Aaron don't do that?'

'Because I know. I would know that kind of shit. Aaron talks to me, right? We're pretty close.'

'I mean, where would it have been better for Elijah to piss?'

'I'm not naive, Myra.'

'What's wrong with some piss? It comes out of everyone.' I was trying to make her laugh. The ravine was electrically green. 'I mean, the shock of it shocked me. Fuck, come on, Lee. Why are you upset?'

Lee rolled another joint. 'You didn't *ask* to be pissed on.'

'Yeah, so? Come on. How the fuck are you supposed to ask someone to piss on you?'

Lee sucked in like a horse. 'A woman can ask for anything she wants.'

She didn't pass me the joint.

'Yeah, well, I don't know … '

Lee looked at me, eyes bulging, fluorescent. 'You don't know what?'

'I found out I liked it even if I didn't ask for it. *You* said that. You're the one who said it was okay for me to want these kinds of things to be true.'

'Well, that's not what I was saying. That's not what I meant.'

'Can I have some, please?'

Lee held in her smoke for as long as she could and then breathed it out slowly, like the line of a song in the air.

'You didn't know this guy's motives, am I right? I mean, you still don't know why he did it. Not just the piss, but like why did this guy want to be with you in his place when he already had a girlfriend. What about her? I mean she was there, right?'

'No.'

'Don't lie, come on.'

'No. She wasn't there when he pissed on me.'

Lee finally passed me the joint, shrivelled and halved. I smoked and I thought. Smoking was good for thinking. I had scrubbed my whole face for Elijah with chamomile soap. I still used toothpaste on the last little bumps on my cheek. Lee had never commented on either my cheek or my makeup. My father, who'd come up from his lair in the basement for takeout, had coughed in shock when he saw me without makeup. 'I told your mother you had to go to the doctor about that,' he said. 'No one ever listens to me.'

'I went to Bernhard *twice*,' I told him. 'Anyway, it doesn't hurt anymore.'

Then my father the zombie surprised me. 'Your friend Jen called here,' he said. 'She told me about some kind of disturbance outside your school. She said a man was with you, a man she didn't know.'

'God. I can't believe she called you. *She's* the disturbance.'

'She was worried, Myra.'

My dad was drowning in his pyjama pants.

'Myra, listen. Your friend was crying on the phone. She said that the man threatened her and Charlene. *Who* are they talking about?'

I started laughing. Like, all of a sudden I'm going to tell my dad things? Just because my mom's not here he wants to have a relationship?

'Next time Jen calls, you can tell her to mind her own fucking house.' I wasn't worried about swearing around him now.

My father stamped his foot on the carpet. It was the most alive I'd seen him in a while.

I tried to hold in my smoke like Lee, to control it like she did coming out, but I coughed and coughed and it all came out flat.

'You know, I had this feeling that first time we met that you were going through something really heavy,' Lee said. 'Aaron did too. I mean, he's really discerning. He's an autodidact. He only likes girls with brains.'

I handed back the J to Lee. A dog barked somewhere far off.

'This is what I think,' Lee said. Then she waited for silence, until a buzzing sound stopped. 'Girls are completely naturally receptive. Someone so receptive is easy to be silenced. I mean, our openness can get fucking crushed.'

'You know what just occurred to me?'

'What?'

'Birds don't chirp at night.'

'Fuck, man. You've got to speak up with guys, Myra. It's frustrating. You're allowed to speak up, you know. Fucking *give* it to them.'

I wasn't tough like Lee was. I wasn't as blunt or succinct. Being stoned with her in the ravine made me feel shy but poetic, like I could light a match inside myself and see what it was that I even wanted to ask for.

'I was willing in that motel room, you know. I was open like a book.'

'Yeah?' Lee seemed impressed for a moment. 'Well, I think some of us are even more open than that.'

I knew what she was talking about. Lee and Wils were best friends and lovers. From the little I'd seen, their relationship seemed really open, like they could tell each other anything. It wasn't like how I'd seen Jen be with her boyfriends, coy and always scheming. The problem for me was that I didn't want Aaron. I wanted Elijah. I wanted to be pissed on. I wanted to enact all my porn.

I'd be more open than a book too. My spine would crack, I'd fall out in halves.

I wanted to say that to Lee, but the moment had passed.

§

I walked into Filmore's Hotel, a four-storey brick building with a painted-black front. In the windows, oblong, hung thick orange curtains. There were seagulls yelling at the edge of the roof.

The reception was empty inside, enclosed in glass. An orange couch with an ashtray beside it was frayed at the bottom and cloud-shape stained.

Filmore's was in the east end of the city, near the place where the streetcar tracks curved. A car had slowed down as I walked up to the hotel and a man rolled down his window on the passenger side: 'You need a lift?' The guy was older, with a beard, he looked like a dentist or something. I was wearing my shortest pink skirt, my white boots, my jean jacket.

'I don't need a lift, thanks.'

I was practising my practice, Lee's practice, of saying what I was thinking. Of being succinct, 'giving it' to men. You are supposed to ask for what you need, Lee had said. What do I need? I need this man to drive off and leave me alone. I need to be inside the hotel. I need to see my beautiful Elijah, a musician who I met in Key West. I need to be dirty for him on my knees.

I am asking to lose my virginity.

I walked past the reception, up two flights of carpeted stairs and down a nicotine-stinked hallway of painted brown doors. Every door had these longish Y-shaped gold handles and a tiny ringed eye in the centre for seeing out. A pattern of cigarette burns struck the wall outside Room 316. At the end of the hallway there was a fire exit and a grey windowpane. I walked the whole length of the hallway to get to his room, 303.

I knocked once. No one answered. The Y-shaped gold handle had a slit in the centre. I was about to knock again.

Elijah opened. His hair was out of his turban, it was electric, in all four directions. He was half-naked, a pair of blue underwear shorts. He looked ready for this. I felt my uncovered cheek.

It was finally time and I wanted to scream: I'm ready I'm ready I'm ready for this!

'I can't believe you came here,' I said. 'I didn't think you'd actually travel all this way up here and I was waiting for you, I waited for you!'

I felt like a child, so serious and eager, finally asking for what I wanted.

'I seriously, seriously never wanted to do anything with anyone until we saw each other again, I mean, I want to come in, let me in, I want to come in there and see you!'

Elijah touched his chest, smiling.

'She ready?' A voice croaked from inside the room.

I took a step backwards. That woman was here.

(GAYL: Sorry for interrupting. But yeah, that was me. I was there with my man in your sin-infested city. We hitchhiked all the way. I didn't realize you Canadians were wallowing in sin.)

'Who is that?'

'My girl Gayl,' Elijah said. Now his smile felt mean.

I turned to go back down the hallway. I felt my thighs under my skirt. 'I thought you were going to come up alone!'

Elijah came out after me, walking faster than my running. At the dirty cigarette burns he got me and pushed my back up against the wall. The ceiling was buckling. It felt too close to my head.

'Don't you leave,' Elijah whispered, his face right up in mine.

'But I thought you were going to come up alone!' I was crying, not looking at him.

'I came this far.'

'I thought you wanted to see me!' I was really trying to wrench myself away.

'I did. I did. I like what I see.' He was blurry. His palms pinned my shoulders.

'You lied. You said you wanted to see me and touch me.'

'Come back to our room.'

'No!' I was struggling but he was stronger than me. Elijah dropped his head into my neck. He rubbed his sharp locks on me, butting forward. I squirmed around and he was sweating and shushing my noises or whatever they were.

'I'm here,' he whispered. 'It's okay, I'm right here.'

But I squealed because I was choking. The necklace he made me became too tight. I tried to push him off me so I could scream. Hot and red from not breathing, I felt Elijah's finger. He reached into the space where the leather cut my throat. My talisman against violence. He ripped it right off. It pinged against the wall. When a talisman breaks into pieces it's a terrible sign. I wanted to scream for my wayward mother. Elijah put his hand on my mouth. An old woman stuck her head out into the hallway to see what was going on.

'You have to shut up,' Elijah said calmly.

My Rastafarian talisman against violence was gone.

I had a man's salty palm on my mouth. I couldn't keep my voice asking for what I needed strong.

LEE: *Shit.* Now it's my turn. I have nothing to say.

§

Jen and Charlene were threatening me. Jen sent me an email saying that she'd had no choice but to call my father. She wrote that if I didn't talk to her about that guy on the street that she was going to call my father again and tell him exactly what Charlene saw. *I miss you, Myra. I wanna drink with you again and we can talk about what is going on.*

What a fucking contradiction. I didn't write back. That made her mad.

Charlene stepped it up in another email: *It's racist, Myra. It's totally fucked up what you did with that black dude. He looks crazy and I'm gonna tell your dad what you did even if Jen won't.*

Right. I was racist. What the fucking fuck.

Then came their final joint email, a multiplication of lies: *That weird dude followed us after he left you. He was calling us beautiful and telling us to come to his hotel. He's a fucking perv, Myra. Just sayin'. You should be careful.*

There were only two more months of school till summer. Ms. Bain and Mr. Rotowsky, my History and English teachers, called me in for a meeting at lunch. Ms. Bain said they were sorry to hear about my mom. It was totally embarrassing. I looked at the floor. I couldn't believe that my dad called the school, that he would've told them about *that*. Then Ms. Bain said that she understood that finishing school would be hard for me this year and so she offered, along with Mr. Rotowsky, that I could hand in one joint essay assignment for them both instead of doing tests and taking final exams.

'You will still need to attend my class,' said Ms. Bain, acknowledging that I'd only been there once since March Break. 'We're on Asia next week. The Japanese-Korean war.'

'And I expect you will not skip my class either,' Mr. Rotowsky added. We'd been reading the Beat Poets in his class, Ferlinghetti and Ginsberg. 'I want you to use this academic opportunity for your benefit, Myra.'

'I will,' I said. Because I knew immediately what I wanted to write about. I was going to write about those Korean sex slaves, like in that book my mother had been reading in Key West. We were on the Japanese-Korean war. My mother was lost in Korea. *Testimonies of the Comfort Women* was about sixteen-year-old girls being taken from their homes and raped by soldiers repeatedly. The rationale of the Japanese government was that their soldiers needed women for sex, sex was comfort in times of war. I was going to connect the Korean sex slaves to the stuff that Aaron had been lending me, like Giorgio Agamben, *Remnants of Auschwitz*, and Georges Bataille, *Inner Experience*. I wanted to write about women and slaves. I mean, in a harrowing life-or-death situation, do people, essentially, have to become slaves? Aaron said that all the European intellectuals were now into Agamben, that they were creating radical cells and writing communally. Aaron said that communal writing was the way of the future. Stoned in Aaron's room, I read Agamben's whole book about the Holocaust, about the Jewish slaves in concentration camps, about these half-dead, half-alive people who were called *Muselmann*. What would have happened if the Korean comfort women could have written communally while they were enslaved? And what about the porn girls? Were those teenage-looking girls in my porn clips slaves? I remembered that exhibition from our trip to Key West, The Last of the Slave Ships. The chains around the people's feet, those emaciated slaves. My mother had been more disturbed than me. I knew how to get my porn clips from the net now by subject. I ordered sado-masochistic porn: *Teengirltied, Ballandcunt, Slutinchains*. The Japanese soldiers raped the Korean comfort women, who were now demanding compensation. How could you compensate a slave? Why did I want to be Elijah's slave?

I felt like I was in a tornado, squeezed so high that I could barely breathe.

§

Elijah had one arm around my waist, one hand on my mouth. The orange curtains in their room were woolly, no light came through from the street. I heard the shriek of the gulls above us on the roof. There was a broken chain lock on the inside of the door. I had been completely subdued.

That woman who slapped me in Key West lay with spread legs on the bed in an old white poncho. The tassels were dirty and full of knots.

'We thought it was going to be cooler up here,' she said, looking at my skirt, how short it was.

I remembered her grinding and coming in Key West. I remembered the blood on her robe in the shape of a lake. Her two-eyed breasts, her full-handed slap. Elijah ate her out in Key West.

I knew that she could tell I'd been crying. Elijah's palm was so big it covered my nose. Three burlap sacks were lined up against the wall.

'This is Gayl,' Elijah said. 'Gayl, meet Myra.'

'You still have that pretty pink bathing suit with the holes in the sides?'

My pink bathing suit had shrunk in the dryer. I didn't know that you weren't supposed to put spandex into heat. My mother had never taught me about laundry. Now it was ruined, a thing for a doll.

'What's the matter with her? She shy or depressed? She looks shocked, E. Kind of a good look.'

Elijah took me to the bed that was a foot away from Gayl's. His palm left my mouth.

I tried not to look at her straight. Gayl's hair was not the same as it had been before. It was more prominent now: two thick brown coils over her ears like headphones.

'Yeah, anyway, she's fine,' Gayl said. 'I don't know what I was thinking.'

I tried not to show my confusion. Gayl was thinner than I remembered, but still those big breasts. She breathed kind of raspy and full so I could hear it. The carpet in their room was colourless. There was a wobbly kitchen table with a hot plate in the corner.

'We're certainly glad you could join us, Mira,' Gayl said, overly friendly.

'It's Myra.'

'Myyyyra? Okay. Yeah, E., she's not afraid to speak her mind. Very nice.'

I didn't understand why she was here and evaluating me and why Elijah was silent about it.

'So what do you got to say for yourself, my Myra? You ready for a ride or what?'

Gayl patted the bed beside her. I sat down. I had a rock in my throat.

Elijah was at the rusty kitchen table with a big brown liquor-store bag.

'I'm, um, busy at school,' I said to Gayl, feeling brave. 'Uh, just doing homework and stuff.'

'Yeah? You studying the classics?'

'No.'

'Good. The Brontës are bullshit.'

I laughed.

'I read Flannery O'Connor back in the day.'

I didn't know who that was. I'd have to ask Aaron.

Elijah handed me red wine in a chipped coffee mug. It was like everything was regular for a second between us, like we were all around the same age and I was just visiting two friends. It felt kind of amazing to swing so fast from fear of her to ease.

I sipped the wine. Elijah began to unpack. Gayl sat up, almost robotically, and she moved off the bed and followed Elijah. She took out piles of clothes from one of the burlap sacks on the floor and shoved them into drawers inside a bureau in the closet. Neither of them touched one of the bags. It looked bulky with a stereo or something.

I considered leaving even though I was calm, even though everything seemed all right. Both of them were ignoring me. I could've just called Lee and told her to come meet me downtown.

Then, as abruptly as they'd started unpacking, they stopped. Gayl resumed her position on the bed I was on. Elijah poured me a second mug of wine. He filled it right to the top. I soaked my lips. Gayl watched me, smiling.

'Look at her. She's a bloodsucker,' Gayl said to Elijah. 'And she was such a tight jailbait shit in the Key.'

My cheek started itching. Elijah winked. I remembered seeing them together, his head slipping around on her body, his tongue pushing up in her pussy. I'd seen that a million times now in porn. *Don't do that to anyone else*, Gayl had said. I wanted to feel that, feel him eat me too.

Elijah motioned me towards him. He had something in his hand. Gayl was watching us but she didn't seem upset. I don't even know why I assumed she'd be jealous. I should have been jealous. I don't think I was jealous.

'Come closer,' Elijah said. He showed me what he had: a flute that was made of burnt yellow wood with zigzags etched in it with a knife. He turned it around while he held the mouth end.

'We might settle here,' he said. 'Gayl's been sick.'

I turned back to look at Gayl. She'd gone under the covers. I was trying to figure out her body under there. Elijah scratched the hairs of his beard. I heard something whirring, a little like a fan. I stared at the lump of her, unmoving.

'Come,' Elijah whispered. 'Let's leave her alone.'

Elijah had this expression of caring for me. But it was just for a moment before his eyes shifted to Gayl in the bed.

He poured me a third mug of wine. 'Drink up,' he said. He wagged the flute.

I knew this was it. I knew we were finally going to have sex. This is what I had come here for, that *disturbance*.

'You good?' Elijah's hand was on my shoulder, pushing me towards the bathroom. I thought I was going to drop my wine. 'You gonna make me crazy again?'

I made my eyes go like the porn girls' eyes. I made my eyes glassy and rabid and hot.

'Yeah, you're gonna make me lose it, bitch.'

I smiled. Elijah had such a good body, his arms were huge. His eyes were just as needy as mine.

If my father knew I was here he would've called the police. Being a bitch in a dirty motel, feeling my ass move side to side in my skirt with a man who was twenty years older than me.

Elijah left the bathroom door open a crack. The light was fluorescent. Elijah's dreadlocks fell out to each side and seemed to separate his face in two, as if he had a good face and a bad face. The tiles were swirly mother-of-pearl. The grout around them grew flowers of rust. I looked up at the ceiling, a buzzing white tube hung from two tiny chains.

'You scared?' Elijah looked behind me towards the crack in the door.

I was totally wet. I liked both of his faces.

'That's okay, Angel. Come right here. Come to me.'

I didn't feel degraded. It occurred to me that an angel could not be degraded.

'We'll go slow,' Elijah said, gripping my arm. 'It's been a long time.'

I was finally where I wanted to be. In a bathroom alone with this man who I wanted so bad. His hand squeezing my arm made me rush, anticipating it. Gayl, his girlfriend, was in the other room. I felt wild. She hated me.

LEE: You've got to be careful about a woman who hates you. Women are vengeful fuckers. Powerless women, completely the worst.

GAYL: Powerless? Who're you calling powerless?

LEE: Look, it's not personal. It's systemic. Systemic oppression inherited from generations of our people being enslaved. It's made us ruthless and vengeful, ideally. I'm a black woman too, you know. My mom's from Zimbabwe.

GAYL: Well, your theory is bunk 'cause I'm an artist. An artist from Kentucky. Artists don't count.

§

Lee read the first draft of my essay in the ravine, under our light. I titled it 'Sex Slaves: The Modern, the Foreign, the Free.' I was trying to prove that all slaves are ashamed but that within this shame there is the potential to be free. I was echoing Agamben, I think, and trying to challenge the historical information about slaves which says that they are ashamed and subjugated, thus they can't ever be unashamed or free.

Slaves, it seemed to me, had secrets, secret lives.

I was expanding the definition of slave to suggest that there *was* such a thing as being enslaved and being free. I remembered the exploitative exhibition I saw with my mother in Key West. It was exploitative because it was totally from the viewpoint of the oppressors, not the slaves. So far I knew that slaves were ashamed, or portrayed as ashamed, because a) they had no freedom, b) they were enmeshed in wars and c) they were always kept apart and alienated from each other. Ms. Bain always told us that we needed to know our conclusion before we even started to write, that that was how you proved something, by working backwards from the conclusion. But my questions were serpentine, inconclusive: What if slaves were not kept apart from each other? What if slaves could take pleasure while enslaved?

My essay was getting more confused as I wrote it. Slaves can have a freedom within shame, I thought, if they create their own subjectivity. Agamben wrote that shame was 'the most proper emotive tonality of subjectivity.' (I felt like Ms. Bain would think that I didn't understand that quote but Mr. Rotowsky would probably give me the benefit of the doubt.) I really did understand it, that emotive tonality. Because slaves can experience pleasure self-consciously, in secret, I wrote. And it is ironic that we see this displayed in contemporary porno-graphic actresses who subvert, very publicly, the notion that slaves are not supposed to feel pleasure. Modern-day slavery is different than slavery in the past. Slavery, I proposed, needs to be re-thought from the contradictory knowledge and expression of shame.

'So, it's just a first draft,' I told Lee. 'It's kind of all over the place, I know.'

Lee was smoking pot. She told me she smoked first thing in the morning sometimes.

'You have to check out the master-slave dialectic.'

'What's that?'

'Oh man, I'm not gonna spoil it for you!'

It occurred to me right then that a master was specific, that not every slave had their own master to love or to hate.

'I want to give this to Chris,' Lee said. Chris being, of course, the legendary dealer that she and Aaron worked for. 'Maybe he can publish it in one of his anarchist rags – they're American, you know.'

'It's not ready for that.'

'Why not? It's pretty good, even without the dialectic.'

Lee held on to my essay. She didn't pass it back. '*Don't*, okay?'

'But you gotta ship out the goods sometimes. You're a good writer, Myra. You should keep doing it. Have you shown this to Aaron? He'd like the way you quoted Agamben. You should acknowledge the way he's educating you.'

The light green-washed Lee's beauty marks. It coloured the smoke streaming out of her nose.

'Uh … It kind of bugs me that you just said that.'

'Why?'

'I'm not a blank slate, you know. I'm not just there to be educated. I read too. I wrote this.'

'Myra. Come on, I *know* you wrote this. I just read it. I think it's amazing. You write kind of rhythmically and it's totally creative. I wasn't doing shit like this in high school. I hope your teachers recognize that. And give you A plus plus plus plus.'

Lee passed me the joint. The joint shut me up.

§

'Hey, Angel.'

'Yeah?'

I wasn't sure what to do, what he wanted.

'Pull down your pants.'

Elijah started playing his flute. It was fast, pointy, climbing the walls.

'Pull down your pants and piss for me.'

That flute was a twig that someone had gored to make sound.

'Go ahead. Do it.'

Elijah looked at me through the mirror. He stopped playing. I pulled my skirt down and sat on the toilet. I didn't take off my underwear.

'And put your finger in the stream.'

'No,' I said.

'Please, Angel. Come on. I want you to do it.'

I imagined Lee saying, You're not dumb! Go!

Elijah crouched down in front of my thighs. His head was almost half my body. Why would I go? Why would I go now? I could touch his hair, his pulsing neck. His lips in the middle of his black beard, blooming. Elijah stared between my thighs at my underwear. I felt them getting wet. I didn't know what to do.

'You're ready now?'

His voice was soft. I nodded.

Elijah touched the head of his flute to my gut.

'Don't,' I said. But it felt okay. Elijah pressed my stomach harder. It hurt just a little. I felt like I had to piss.

'You can go,' he said.

'I don't have to. I really don't.'

Then Elijah traced the flute up underneath my shirt. He drew a line with it through my breasts. From under my shirt it went to my lips. He touched my lips with the head of the flute. It was damp from his mouth. He started opening my lips.

I was going to say *don't* again but Elijah used my open mouth as a chance to go in. The flute was a prod. My lips hardened around it.

'Relax them.'

I did it. I relaxed. Then I heard a sound, like a fan just turned on.

Elijah pushed in and out of my mouth with the flute. My T-shirt got pulled away from my body like a tent. There was friction. He could see everything. I felt my lips soften but I was still sucking. I let the flute move in and out of my lips, under my shirt. I closed my eyes and I knew he was looking. He was looking at me with that flute fucking in and out of my mouth. And then I couldn't help it, with it pressing on my tongue, so relaxed I wanted to say *guh*, I started peeing right through my underwear. I put my hand there to stop it but I couldn't stop it.

The flute poked and twirled faster. Elijah's breath was metallic, right at my neck. 'I told you to come. That's it. I told you to come.' I spasmed. It all went too fast. I was still pissing when I came. My throat felt like a balloon. I wanted it out of me, coughing.

'What am I gonna do, what am I gonna do?' It was hard to speak right. 'My underwear's wet.'

Elijah helped me stand. I felt totally weak. I let him work off my skirt and my soaking underpants. Elijah got some toilet paper and he wiped me like I was a child. My knees started to bend. He held me up by the armpits.

'I missed you,' he said.

I had never been so close to a man. I'd never been able to be right there, and his smell, his sweat, the metal root smell of his breath and him helping me. Elijah had to balance me up against the sink. Then he closed the bathroom door with his foot. The door stuck on something. My lips were open, my eyes were closed, I was trying to swallow to stop any tears.

Elijah whispered up at my ear: 'Would you come places with me if I asked you to?'

'Yeah,' I heard myself saying. 'I'll go anywhere, anywhere with you.'

I opened my mouth. I had to kiss him alive. I had my tongue in his mouth and I was sticking to him. It was all happening to me, it was finally happening. I moved around my tongue, we were kissing and dancing. I rubbed my red cheek onto his beard. Elijah moved his hands to take off his pants, with one foot sliding off his shorts. The lights were so bright in that bathroom. I wanted the flute again. I only wanted him. I wanted what he wanted. Elijah had the flute in one hand and he was holding me where I was with the other. I looked down at his legs as we were kissing, his two long naked thighs and cock low like a stick. Tears globbed and swelled at the top of my throat. Elijah pressed his thighs into mine. His purple-brown cock underneath all the hair. I could see how it was charging. I wanted to hold it. But Elijah slipped the flute between my thighs. He started rolling it back and forth so the middle almost kept slipping inside me. I made sounds like cracks that I couldn't control. The sink pushed into my back, forming a bruise.

'You have to be in the right place,' Elijah whispered, straining, as he twisted the head of the flute. 'I'm trying to help you.'

It was uncomfortable and I couldn't breathe right. I looked down between his naked chest and my T-shirt: his fist upturned, half of the flute. His cock was twice the size of the flute.

'I'm gonna stick it up there as far as it'll go.'

I was not held up by my feet anymore but his knees pressing into my thighs.

'Take your hand off the sink and rub yourself now,' Elijah sounded tense. 'Take your hand and touch yourself.'

I squeezed my hand down between us. I didn't know why he wanted me to do that right now. I heard something outside the bathroom door. I was terrified Gayl was going to walk in. I stared at the doorknob, it wasn't moving.

'Forget it, forget it. Rub in a circle.'

I'd already come and I felt too raw to do it.

'Go on, keep on rubbing. That's good.'

Elijah was smiling at what I was doing.

'Say you're my bitch.'

'Uh?'

'Say you're my little bitch.'

The wooden flute was all the way inside me. It felt good one second, then it felt stuck.

'Come on, say you're my dirty little bitch.'

As my knees softened the flute got higher.

'Say it. Say it.'

'I'm your, I'm your little dirty … '

Elijah licked in my ear. 'Yeah like that … '

'Bitch.'

Oh god, that felt good! His tongue in my ear.

My head dropped back and now I was really feeling something, the flute in my body, a dog humping desperate, a bitch on the floor. I grabbed up and pumped. My hips moved side to side, it pushed in me hard and forward and I pulled and wiggled back. I felt myself making fire like that. Then my whole body clamped and a bark left my jaw.

The bathroom went dark. I was floating, my arms and legs full of needles. I dissolved to the floor. The flute rattled there.

'Elijah,' I whispered, feeling for his feet. 'Turn on the light.'

'Shh, I'm right here.'

'Turn on the light!'

I heard a small bell, a ping. My necklace had pinged. It was gone, in the hallway.

'Please! Turn it on!'

Something bad was going to happen. I felt his hands on my head. How'd he see where I was? I couldn't see. I held on to his wrist and he lifted me up. Then Elijah hugged me.

'We don't need the light,' he said.

We were shadows touching. I wanted it to last. I closed my eyes, putting darkness on top of darkness, and breathed our smells being mixed together.

I took a picture like that of the two of us together, locked in the bathroom, locked in this hotel so that I would always smell this: rosehip, caramel, the fountain of piss.

We were encased, intertwined in silence for a while.

§

'Dad, Jeff, this is Lee.'

Jeff stared at Lee like she was trapped behind glass. She wore the same fuzzy red sweater as when I first met her. My dad still thought that Jen and Charlene were my friends. He had on jeans and a button-down. He wasn't saying anything.

'Dad … '

'I'm Myra's father. Neil. Call me Neil. Sorry. Please.'

Lee looked my father in the eyes. 'It's really great to meet you, Neil.'

'Yes, yes, you too. So what do you do, Lee? Myra hasn't told me anything about you.'

'I'm in between jobs,' Lee said, totally at ease. 'But I'd like to be an editor one day. I work with Aaron too.'

My father glanced at me.

'Uh, Aaron is Jeremy Copter's brother. Jeremy from my school. He's friends with Jen and Charlene and those guys. We hang out sometimes.'

'Oh. Okay,' my father said. He seemed disoriented.

The doorbell rang. Jeff ran for the door and my father left us to pay the pizza delivery guy. The table was dirty. It hadn't been wiped in a week.

'Your father seems nice,' Lee said. 'Concerned.'

'He wasn't always. It's changing. I mean, since my mom left.'

Jeff brought the pizza to the table, holding it high in the air. My dad offered Lee a glass of wine. 'You're of age, I take it?'

'I'm okay,' Lee smiled.

'I'll have a glass,' I said. I felt embarrassed by my father and Lee talking to each other.

My father visited our liquor cabinet in the living room and returned with a bottle and three fancy glasses – the full-bowled ones with the really long stems.

'This is a burgundy,' he said. 'The good stuff.'

'Cool!'

'Your mother and I brought this bottle back from our final trip to Europe.'

'When you and Jody had that party,' Jeff piped in.

'Oh yes,' said my dad, looking at me.

Final trip, I thought.

'Our neighbours called the cops,' Jeff explained to Lee. 'I slept through the entire thing!'

'Apparently it was a very, *very* good party,' my father added, moving his eyebrows up and down, like he used to.

'Why?' Lee asked.

'Myra's friend Jen threw up sangria, was that sangria? I remember orange pulp in a beautiful cloud burned into our good white couch, which we had to throw out and, if I remember correctly, the police were called ... '

My father paused for effect.

'*Dad.*' I didn't want him to go on. I knew he was trying to be funny. But it was like my father was drunk without even opening the bottle.

'Lee, have you met our Jody yet?'

'No,' I hissed. 'Lee hasn't met Jody.' Jody would have fucking killed my father for this.

'Wine sounds good,' Lee said. She smiled at me. 'Okay?'

The music had been cranked up so loud at that party that no one had even heard the door. The police barged in, there were four of them and they were shouting at everyone. No one thought to turn down the music so it was on the entire time they were there, checking every single room, confiscating every single bottle. I was with Jen and Charlene in my room, sharing a mickey. I didn't even know that Jen had already thrown up. Apparently the police found Jody naked in our parents' room with three university guys. That was written up in the report so my parents found out. They had to pay this massive fine for underage drinking. They didn't even know that Jody was on the pill.

My dad poured three full glasses of the burgundy. I reached across the table for mine.

'Hang on,' Lee said. 'Let me make a toast.'

Lee looked at me and nodded. I felt so strange.

'To Neil, to Myra, to Jeff and to Jody *in absentia.*' Lee looked up at our alien light fixture that hung over the steaming pizza box. 'Thank you for this food and this company and being in the moment. Chin-chin.'

Jeff started laughing. 'Chin-chin?'

I downed my wobbly glass. 'Chin-chin! Thank you, Father, for that final trip!'

My father sipped his wine and ignored me. 'Cheers. Thank you, Lee. It's been a while since I've had anything to drink.'

'This is really, really good,' Lee said.

'Yep. My mother knows her grape,' I said. 'Wonder what she's drinking in Seoul. She's in Seoul, right?'

My father peeled his pepperonis off his slice and ate them first. 'Yes, Myra,' he said. 'We all know that.'

I wolfed down three slices. Lee seemed uncomfortable and ate really slowly. Jeff read his manga over dinner. I wanted more wine.

'Is that Sailor Moon?' Lee tipped up the cover of Jeff's book. 'It's cool that you read shojo. Vintage too! You should check out *Rose of Versailles* – Oscar's a fucking maniac bisexual. Sorry, 'scuse my language.'

Jeff laughed. So did my dad. 'No, no, it's okay, Lee. My daughter is a champion cusser.'

'Cusser?' Cusser sounded like one of my video clips. *Teenslut-cusserlicker*.

'Cusser, like cuss words. You don't know that term?'

'I know that term, Dad, but I didn't think I was a cusser. I just thought I was a freak.'

'No, Myra, come on. You're not ... '

I don't know why I felt like crying. My mouth swarmed with cheese grease.

'Cusser sounds cool,' said Jeff. 'I wanna be a cusser too. How do I get *Rose of Versailles*?'

'Call me,' Lee said. 'I have a digest compilation of the first year. Call and I'll bring it to you after school or something one day.'

Lee ripped a piece of the empty pizza box and she wrote down her number on the back. Jeff, I thought, blushed. My father stood up and stuck Lee's cardboard number on the fridge with a magnet. I felt my gut, the pizza, the flute in my gut.

'Have a good time, kids,' my father said later, tipsy, framed by the door. 'Next time you can invite Aaron too. What do you say, Myra?'

Lee answered for me. She was definitely not a kid. 'Okay, Neil. It was great to meet you. Bye, Jeff!'

I galloped down the porch stairs. My father, alone and gaunt from the house light behind him, watched me and Lee crawl into Aaron's car.

Aaron kissed me open-mouthed in the front seat. His tongue was lukewarm.

'Mmmmmm, you girls hittin' the sauce with your dad?'

'A glass, just a glass.'

Aaron backed out of our driveway. The light in Jeff's room went on. I hoped my father hadn't seen me and Aaron.

Chris's party was in the east end of the city. I knew we'd be passing by Filmore's. I was thinking about how I'd get there later, after this party that was supposed to be so important. I'd called Elijah's room and he hadn't answered.

'So ... Lee says she gave Chris your opus.' Aaron squeezed my thigh too hard and I jumped. 'When am I gonna get to read it too?'

'I can't believe you did that. Lee! That was my fucking first draft!'

Lee and Wils were making out in the back seat. Wils waved his hand at me, as in: go away. They kept kissing. I couldn't believe she did that. And that she was fucking ignoring me.

'My, my, Myra, don't stress.' Aaron wove in and out of the streetcar tracks. 'Chris is open. He's got a lot of connections. He's starting the university tonight, right, Wils? Like, modelled on the free-school movement of the sixties. Maybe he'll discuss your essay or something.'

Aaron jammed on the gas to get around every car he could.

'I don't know,' Wils said, his mouth half in a kiss. 'Ask this one. She's the expert.'

'I just thought Chris would want to read it,' Lee said quietly. 'Shows how much I admired it, right?'

My essay had stalled. I could not imagine this Chris or Ms. Bain or Mr. Rotowsky reading it and passing me. I was getting more sucked into the internet porn and there was less and less of a connection with the comfort women, or any other historical aspect, like the last slave ships to land at Key West. Everything was changing and stalled because of the master-slave dialectic, because of Hegel. I believed that everyone now, not just pornographic actresses or the *Muselmänner*, but everyone, according to Hegelian dialectic, was on the continuum of being a slave. 'The Master-Slave dialectic describes in narrative form the encounter between two self-conscious beings,' I read on Wikipedia, 'who engage in a struggle to the death before one enslaves the other – only to find that this does not give him the control over the world that he sought.'

The slave's self-consciousness, according to Hegel, *not* the master's, sublates into Absolute Knowledge.

This was changing everything for me. Sublation meant cancelling out and preservation; both, together, at the same time. You could get rid of something and protect it too. I realized that I wanted to sublate myself to Elijah. I wanted to be consumed by him and elevated by him and preserved in the process. I didn't know how to do this. This didn't seem inevitable. Did I have to struggle to the death? And what about Gayl?

I heard sounds from the back seat of the car, grunts being stifled. Lee's grunts. I started thinking about Gayl.

'Who is Flannery O'Connor, you guys?'

'Oh yeah, my girl Flannery!' Aaron shouted. The whole car shifted left. A streetcar beeped and we jerked in front of it. Lee screamed and then laughed, getting off on Aaron's speed.

'Take it easy back there, dudes!' Aaron shouted.

Aaron had his little bag full of drugs on his lap. It was a circle of red leather with a zipper that went all the way around. He lit a joint, I think to distract himself.

'Flannery O'Connor, Myra, is one strange-ass lady writer. She described violence in a way that no one ever had before. I've got some of her collections. She's from Savannah. That's the south.'

I held on to the door handle as Aaron shifted off the streetcar tracks so we could go even faster. In my side-door mirror I didn't see Lee anymore. Wils' eyes were closed.

Aaron passed me the J. I took a few hard long puffs. Wils' shoulders were moving. I heard Lee breathing through her nose.

I didn't want to lose my virginity with Aaron.

'Flannery O'Connor had no sex life. Which probably helped her writing. Don't you think?'

'Oh yeah!' Lee sat up and wiped her mouth. Wils stretched his arm right out the window and laughed. I felt Lee's eyes in the back of my head.

'Can I have some of that, Aar?'

'Ask Myra. She's the fiend tonight.'

'Myra, can I please pretty please have some of that?'

I stuck my arm backwards. Lee held my wrist. She sucked in from the joint with me holding it. I knew I was just supposed to forgive her. Maybe she really did think my essay was brilliant. Maybe this guy Chris would actually publish it when I was done.

'Have you tried X yet, Myra?' Wils asked from the back.

'No.'

'You gotta try it, it's excellent.'

'True,' Lee added. 'She should try it one day. But, Myra, you know, she's already ecstatic.'

We passed by Filmore's Hotel. I looked up. Elijah's light was not on. I wanted him bad. I wanted a sex life. I wanted to be ecstatic. I wanted to be up there in the bathroom giving it to him.

§

Chris's building was small and rundown with long bubbled windows in the front. There were speakers off the second-floor balcony. A couple of guys in ripped jeans waved at us and went inside. One of them was Jeremy, Aaron's brother.

Inside, Lee took me by one arm and Aaron hooked me by the other. I felt like a convict. We made our way like that through the black-painted rooms lit up with candles in bottles.

'This is My-My, everyone,' Aaron said to the last room, a windowless office of ground-to-floor books in crates.

'Myra,' I hissed.

Lee squeezed my arm. 'It's okay,' she whispered.

There was a red-haired, bearded guy perched on a milk-crate throne smiling at us. A group of people sat crossed-legged below him in a circle. Everyone looked pleased to see Aaron with his little red purse.

'It's so nice to meet the writer, finally,' said Chris, the king holding court, stretching out his arm as if we were supposed to go and touch it.

My heart started racing. I forgot that I was stoned.

I had a feeling that Jen and Charlene were here.

I extracted myself from Aaron and Lee and ran out of that black room into the kitchen. Charlene and Jen, yes, were at the table, smoking in aprons. They didn't look surprised to see me. It smelled like garlic roasting. I can't believe that guy read the first draft of my essay. Which sucked. Fucking god.

'Why are you guys here?'

'Aaron's got the best stash,' Jen said. 'That dude Chris is totally hot. And Jeremy invited us, so fuck you, okay?'

I left the kitchen. The fact that that guy had read my essay made me feel hairy, breathy shame.

'Myra! My-ra!' I heard Lee. I kept hearing my name.

The office was packed now with people on the floor and at the walls. Chris's eyes were like those small laser flashlights that can stun you from miles away. Smoke hung low over everyone's heads. Lee was smiling at me. She looked proud.

'Let us welcome our young writer here. Myra, everyone, the partner of Aaron.'

Everyone turned to look at me and clapped. Jen and Charlene were behind me. They were clapping too. I felt sick. Chris stood up. He was short, my height. His T-shirt had a dripping map of the world on it, as if the world were made of blood. In the corner it said: *Fuck off*. I felt a contact high from Chris that was not pot. I squatted low behind Aaron to get away. Lee was right up at the front of the room, near Chris's throne. She looked at Chris kind of deferentially, I thought. He reminded me of a tomcat. I pressed my breasts into Aaron's back on purpose. I could feel him happy that I was doing that, sweating.

'We have an interesting thesis to discuss tonight, everyone. Myra, would you do the honours and introduce your idea?'

I shook my head no. Aaron tried to buck me off him.

'You should,' he whispered.

I shook my head again, but I stood up.

Chris was looking at my body, lasers on my tits. My knees went buttery like they had with Elijah.

'We were going to be discussing Spartacus tonight for our inaugural lecture, the most renegade of slaves.' Chris smiled at me. 'When our good friend Lee happily forwarded me your essay, Myra. It was quite a brilliant coincidence. The revolt of slaves is in the air.'

The revolt of slaves is in the air …

'When Lee told me further, Myra, that you were only sixteen, I'll tell you the truth, I was even more impressed. Your concerns are not vital for a person your age. And yet, in past times, as we know, the teenage girl was an important resource, a medium for struggle. Emma Goldman was radicalized as a young woman your age. Marta too, the first female slave to rise up against the Romans, was only thirteen … So there is a history of fiery young women like yourself.'

Fiery? I started laughing. Did the tomcat want me to strip in the centre of flames?

'So, Myra, please tell us your thoughts.'

Shame smashed together with shame. I just stood there. Wished we could talk about Hegel: the master in love with the slave and the slave with the master, a circle, until the master was slave and slave had her power. Chris lit a joint. I liked his red beard. What about multiple slaves in love with one master?

Aaron stood up. 'Myra's kind of shy but she's read a lot. Agamben and Weil, for starters, right, My?'

I felt suddenly pissed off at Aaron and Lee for putting me in this position. I was not a blank slate. Slaves revolt.

'I read about porn stars,' I said.

Jen and Charlene started cracking up behind me.

'Ah, the vanguard,' Chris said. He thought he knew why I was opposing him.

'There's this cool site I subscribe to called realteenwhores.com.'

'He's cool, Myra, Chris is cool,' Aaron whispered at my ear. 'Want to go wait for me in the kitchen? Me and Lee got business for a sec.'

People started to talk to each other, stand up. Chris raised his hand and in a second everyone was quiet. 'Our newest members, Jen and Charlene, will be making us a meal of sprouted buckwheat burritos,' Chris said. 'Myra, perhaps you should go help them out if you don't want to be a part of our teach-in.'

Everyone looked at me. 'I wouldn't eat what they made,' I said.

Lee guffawed. I didn't care what anyone thought. I just wanted to leave and get to Elijah.

Chris looked amused. 'Break, please, everyone. We'll reconvene after grub. Jen and Charlene, you have my apologies. Myra, wait here.'

Everyone left the little room. Aaron kissed me on the cheek as he left, but it was cold. I knew that he was angry with me. Chris held my essay, which was only four pages. He motioned for me to come over to get it. His arms were thin and bulging with veins.

'Sit down, please, Myra,' Chris said when we were alone. He passed me his joint.

'Yes, sir?' I said, cross-legged in front of him, looking up. I held his green eyes as I sucked in my smoke. It tasted weird, like poppy seeds. It was easy to blow light and upward in a perfect curled line.

'Are you trying to make us laugh or cry in this paper of yours?'

It was as if an arrow shot me in the side. 'Both,' I said.

I was dripping now like his T-shirt, the map of the world. I slid around on the floor so he could see up my skirt.

Chris took a moment. 'See, you're titillating, Myra, if you really need to know that. Which I don't think you do. I think you already know that about yourself.'

Lee touched me on the shoulder. 'Aaron's waiting for us in the car,' she whispered.

'I don't care,' I said.

'We gotta go, c'mon, My.'

'Me and *My* were just talking.'

'Myra,' I said.

'Me and Myra were just talking about what a *titillating asshole* she is.'

'Oh fuck,' Lee said as she reached down for my hand.

I looked up at Lee backwards. Her neck was lifted and long like a swan's.

'It's okay. He's right. Chris was just telling me that I'm tight. He's the second guy to say that to me ... '

'Let's *go*, Myra,' Lee said. She crouched down and hooked me.

'An asshole is tight, it doesn't dilate naturally,' Chris said. He was amused by how much his drug had me crippled. It was hard for us to coordinate, Lee had to help me stand.

'Everything is tight on me,' I said, smiling. 'Maybe you should try and feel that sometime.'

I started to gain clarity. Hairs prickled up on my arms. Jen and Charlene were in the kitchen. They were like my innermost core. I was rebelling against the fucking passivity and privilege and girlishness that was epitomized by them.

'Come back when you're ready, when you're whole,' Chris said. 'I'll feel you, Myra, no problem at all.'

'You'll feel my tight pussy?'

'Oh god,' said Lee.

'No one will experience your brain unless you learn how to listen to people,' Chris said. 'How to even respect your enemies.'

I hadn't wanted anyone to read my essay until I was done.

'My enemies are fucking dependent on me,' I said.

Lee pulled me away from Chris, through the dark hallway and the flickering front room. It felt like a roller-coaster ride. I was laughing. Inside my mouth was the black seedy stink of that joint. Outside, Wils was standing at the car. Aaron was a ghost of smoke in the driver's seat. What I really wanted was to sit in the back seat with Lee. I wanted her to put her arm around me and let me lay my head on her shoulder in the speed. I wanted to fall and fall asleep. The titillating asshole was totally spent.

GAYL: This girl, *damn*. She needs me, she needs me!

LEE: I was trying to take care of her too.

GAYL: Hand her over. She needs real-life. No more of these half-assed, drippy, aborted explorations.

LEE: Aborted? I don't think that friendship and empathy are aborted explorations. Neither is anarchy. It's all a process. You're harsh.

GAYL: Yeah, I'm not into process. I'm from Kentucky. We do washboard justice. Just hand her over. You'll see what I see.

§

Elijah came towards me through the darkness of the bathroom. This was our place to find each other while Gayl was in the other room wrapped up in sheets. Elijah's white robe was a heap on the floor. My hands were tied behind my back with a towel. I was sucking his cock without limbs. I started feeling like my head was my whole self.

'You're such a good cocksucker,' Elijah said.

The two of us were psychic, master and slave. Only the master knows what the slave really wants, no matter how many times she runs away.

There was a ribbon of light from the slit in the door. Elijah grabbed on to the back of my head. He went so deep inside me I started to choke. I tried to turn my cheek to his stomach. My sucking stopped. I couldn't breathe. Elijah was moaning going in me and speeding up my name. When I forced my mouth off him I felt her there, right at the door.

'Don't be scared,' said Elijah, turning me back to him. 'You don't need to be scared.'

Was I scared? I wasn't fucking scared! I let him go back in my mouth. I wanted my wrists tied even tighter, I wanted them tied properly, tied with leather, proper with rope. Then I would open myself more instead of going titillating tight. It's true that only an asshole is tight.

'You're a princess,' Elijah whispered as I sucked for him. He held me up by my hair. 'Exactly like this on your knees. A princess warrior bitch.'

Sweat rose from my back like a carpet alive, it dripped from my armpits, it fired my scalp. In my mouth he was as hard as a rail. My mouth sucked him perfect and my cunt lit up. My mouth and my cunt were completely connected. I could implode and come and come and come.

Elijah's cock shook, then he pulled out and left me completely.

A burning-hot raindrop hit my eye.

His whole body vibrated; both his hands were on his heart. There was pain in my eye, blinding tears. I used his robe to wipe my face.

According to Hegel, the slave fully acknowledges the self-consciousness of the master and she dissolves herself or upholds herself as their relationship dictates and evolves to the struggle unto death. Although this struggle is a failure, according to Hegel, if someone actually dies.

I started laughing. I didn't know why but I felt good.

Elijah hugged me into himself. Curls of his hair down there stuck to my cheeks.

'You're such a good cocksucker,' Elijah said.

I squeezed my eyes shut. The burning didn't leave.

I felt his cock heavy, hanging down at my neck. It seemed like a necklace, a part of my body; for a second, I thought it was mine.

'You can have it,' Elijah said.

I was in a struggle unto death. His cock was my new talisman.

§

The ravine expanded through my tears. My mother missed my birthday. I turned seventeen. My father had ordered an ice-cream cake and sunk eighteen rainbow candles in it. Being eighteen is freedom. It felt like my mother would never be a mother again.

'Your dad's worried about you, Myra. He told me that sometimes you don't come home at night.'

'Just give me a minute.'

I didn't want to be crying anymore. I didn't want my father talking to Lee while I was pissing either.

'You're sensitive,' Lee whispered. 'It's so tender, Myra. Come on, it's really tender. It's so tender it could kill someone.'

I dug in my fingers to the roots of the grass.

'Your mother knows you're sensitive too.'

I cried then, a lot. I thought it had stopped but it hadn't. I felt it on my cheeks, in my throat and deep inside my stomach. I felt like such a female. As if this kind of pain were the wobbling, howling essence of that.

'Don't talk to my dad anymore about anything,' I got out. 'I don't want him to know what I'm doing. He's going to tell Jody and Jody'll tell my mom and I don't want my mother to know fucking anything about me!'

'Okay, Myra. I'm sorry. I won't. I didn't tell him anything. I'll tell him that I can't talk about you if he brings it up. He's just worried, though. Parents get worried. It makes sense.'

Lee didn't know that I'd been with Elijah last night, that if I'd died from our master-slave psychic sex, I would've died satisfied.

'I'm just fucked up,' I said. I started ripping up grass.

'Fucked up about Elijah or your mother?' Lee asked.

I had nothing to say. I wanted sublation.

'Fuck, Myra! You have to be clearer about this! Are you afraid of that guy? Is he hurting you?'

'No. *No.* It's just, masochism, I think.'

Lee lit up a joint. 'Masochism,' she said. 'Right.'

Masochism seemed to make sense to me in terms of the struggle for self-consciousness of the slave in the struggle unto death.

'I feel like sex, I mean giving myself, helps me. Giving my whole self to someone until I forget who I am helps me deal with my problems.'

Lee started laughing. Her laughing made me laugh. 'Sex like that doesn't deal with your problems, it compounds them, you sneaky little shit. It builds on top of the problems you already have!'

It felt good to go straight from crying to laughing. I smeared grass on my jeans.

'Listen, I should tell you something,' Lee said. The whipping night wind blew leaves around us. 'I was molested when I was a kid. That's why I'm so virulent about things.'

'Oh.'

'Sex. I mean, I'm virulent about sex. About the power dynamics.'

'Okay ... '

We stared at each other. Lee didn't move from my gaze, my gaze moved first.

'It was my teacher in Grade 6. I was twelve. She had a crush.'

'You mean a woman molested you?'

'Yeah. You shouldn't be so surprised.'

'Sorry.'

'Don't be sorry. Fuck. I don't know if I can tell you about this now.'

'I'm sorry, really.'

'I'm not like your old friends, you know, Myra.'

'I know.'

'Jen and Charlene are toxic and naive.'

'I know! You're totally right, they are. Lee, come on.'

'I'm not going accept your naïveté like they did, Myra.'

'Okay, I know.'

'You know what?'

'I know what you mean.'

'What do I mean?'

'Jen and Charlene are toxic and naive but they act like they're not. I've been influenced by them. I've been naive. I don't think about things always.'

'Yeah. You don't. You have to work on actually thinking about other people. Other people have a different life from you, Myra. Different pasts, different thoughts. Different ways of fucking managing things. It's frustrating to me, Myra. You're not conscious of that.'

'Okay. I'm sorry.'

'Stop saying you're sorry.'

'Please. Lee. Please tell me what happened to you,' I said quietly. 'I want to know.'

Lee wasn't looking at me. Her breathing was loud. She'd just called me naive. I was tight, titillating, an asshole and naive. I had to remember all these things, qualities of my self-consciousness.

It took Lee another few moments to talk. There was a man walking his dog on the path at the bottom of our hill. He looked in our direction and waved. He watched us for a few seconds before moving on.

'She kept me after school a few times to work on things with her, just cleaning the classroom or whatever, or talking about our class and who I liked and didn't like. I didn't think that much about it, actually – I was just happy to be with her. We analyzed people and that was cool. I felt special, I guess. But then it kind of progressed, if I can use that word, from it just being easy to talk to her about school to her wanting to talk to me about my family, especially about my mom and dad and how much they let me go out and all that. And I talked. I liked her and I told the truth about all of those things. I didn't feel strange about any of the time we spent together until she started telling me one day about herself too, stories about how she went on dates with guys but she didn't ever want to be with anyone. Then she told me she thought the penis was a very ugly organ. She asked me if I'd ever seen a penis before.'

'Wow.'

'I know. Grade 6, right? And I hadn't, of course. So, I think that's where it turned. Nothing happened that day, but it happened pretty soon after that. She capitalized on something, I guess, the fact that I didn't know anything about sex and that I liked talking to her. Because then, this one time, she just admitted it. She said she couldn't help it. She said that she really, really liked me and she didn't want a boyfriend. And she kept asking me all the time if I was okay with that, if I was okay with her feeling things for me like that. And she said if I was uncomfortable, I should just tell her. But the thing was, I wasn't uncomfortable. I liked it, actually, and I liked her too. She told me stuff about herself. She was smart.'

'So, you mean, it was a good experience for you?'

'No. Not really. I mean, that's not a bad question, and it was all pretty good until she started wanting stuff from me. Like, first it was a kiss goodbye on the cheek. Then the double kiss. Okay, once, I remember this really well, after a double kiss she kind of grabbed me by the waist and kept me close. And then she said, "Lee, you have an incredible body. I just think you should know." She didn't let go of my waist when she said that. That was when I really felt that something was happening between us. Something uncontrollable.'

Lee paused. She looked past me.

'I was only twelve, right? So to me, when she said I had an incredible body, I felt like I was hot shit. I had this secret. We started doing more things. I sat on her lap. I let her put her legs between my legs. I used to look at myself naked in my bedroom and think of how she would be seeing it. And I wanted her to see me like that because I felt like I was addicted to that feeling of her saying, *You have an incredible body. I think you should know.* We started kissing more. We got to doing it with our tongues. I let her touch my breasts.'

Lee's cheeks lit up. She looked out, not at me.

'I wore these special loose shirts and this was just when I was getting tits or whatever. I wore them so that she could feel me there, but she never just felt my breasts when she went under my shirt, she always felt everywhere around them, taking so long to get to them. I closed my eyes and sat on her lap, sometimes facing her and sometimes away from her and I'd just sit there so willing and lap up every single second because every single stroke of it felt so good. She knew how much I liked it. She really knew. I was her lapdog. She had so much power over me.'

'Lee … '

'No, listen, this one day we were really going at it, probably the most I'd ever let her do. My pants were opened and it was the first time she was going in my pants. I was going to let her do everything that day, it was seriously the day I knew I was going to let her feel me down there, I'd thought about it endlessly, right? And my shirt was up, she was kissing and licking my breasts and I was holding her too, I was really holding her tight because she was sucking and sucking on my nipples so hard I thought I was going to faint from how good it felt.'

Lee looked at me, an open book.

'Our janitor walks in. He coughs or something. I don't remember being shocked but she, she immediately starts sobbing. Her whole face goes red and she covers it up with her hands. I think she actually fell down on the floor. I still have no idea how she went from doing what she was doing to full-body fucking sobbing. I remember I pulled down my shirt and zipped up my pants. Then I went out with the janitor and I never saw her again.'

Lee took one huge long drag of smoke and let it out to the light.

'See, what I realized later, Myra, I mean not until much, much later – because I was a fucking suicidal mess after she left our school and I had to be examined by psychologists and doctors and shit – was that through that relationship with her, I'd just gone along with her feelings the entire time. I felt a lot and I wanted it, yeah, but essentially I just went along with her desires. First her need to talk to me, and then her need to get me to talk, then her need to touch me and her need to know how I wanted her to touch me. But this whole thing happened without me really understanding what my own needs were, or where they came from. I can admit that. I loved her back, right? Just like she loved me.

'So, it took me all these years to examine what was mine in there. I mean, if she didn't like me first, would I have liked her? Considered her for fucking? I'm being honest. This is the kind of stuff I have to take responsibility for.'

Lee's knee was shaking. I moved my hand there.

§

I woke up to low weeping moans from the bathroom. I was too scared to move.

'What's wrong with her?' I whispered. I didn't know if it was morning.

Gayl started hacking. Elijah stirred and pulled me in close.

'She's having some emotional issues,' Elijah said, breathing in my neck. 'Go back to sleep. The woman is confused.'

'What do you mean?'

'She's not your age, Myra.'

'So?'

'She wants a baby.'

'Oh.'

Elijah laughed. 'But you're all these dark bitches until fifty or sixty.'

I didn't know what the fuck he was talking about. Elijah strapped me in with his arms and tried to stop me from shaking. He was shaking too. I didn't know what to do. The sheets were damp. Gayl's retching and hacking went away. Elijah rubbed my cheek with the cracked tips of his fingers.

I heard a whimper.

'I'm going to check on her.' Elijah rolled away from me. I got cold. After a few seconds I got up out of the bed. Gayl was on the floor in the bathroom, hunched over the toilet. I touched her shoulder.

'Are you okay?'

Tiny hairs were stuck to her forehead with sweat. Her eyes were so heavy that she only looked at me through half of them. They were red-flecked.

'Get yourself out of here,' she said. 'Leave me alone. You should listen to him.'

'Do you need water?'

Gayl laughed and hacked. 'I just got this fucking annoying problem. Did you hear me? Get the fuck out.'

I left her and went back into the bed with Elijah. I lifted up his arm, hid myself under there. 'When you and I make love, it's going to be big,' Elijah whispered.

'What about Gayl?' I asked. Her sweat and sickness and red eyes in there. 'Do you have big sex with her?'

'She can't do it anymore.' Elijah held me even tighter.

My heart flipped. 'What's wrong with her? Why is she so sick in there?'

'Emotional problem, I said.'

Lee would say I was in over my head, that I would have to figure out what my needs were in all this.

'But maybe we should take her to a hospital. She's really really sick.'

Elijah pushed me over to the side of the bed. He sucked his teeth. 'She's got a woman problem. Go tell your daddy.'

'What?'

Gayl started retching again.

'Get out of here, all right? Leave us alone. Can't you hear her? She wants you to leave!'

Elijah closed his eyes. The bathroom door clicked. Both of them had told me to leave.

'What did I do?' I asked. 'Fuck, what'd I just do?'

Elijah didn't open his eyes. 'Don't make me get up,' he said. He didn't care about me. Neither of them cared at all about me. Lee was right, I'd degraded myself.

§

I called Aaron when I got home at three in the morning. He was driving to Barrie with Wils in the car. He answered his phone just by breathing in smoke.

'My, my, Myra,' he said on the exhale.

'Are you ever gonna stop smoking?' I asked him. Female problems where you can't have sex, I looked that up on Wikipedia.

Aaron coughed crap. 'Not gonna stop if I can help it, baby. Why do you ask?'

'Does Wils even like me?' I asked.

'Why do you always want to know about yourself?' Aaron asked back.

'I'm just curious.'

'And narcissistic?'

'Whatever. No.'

I counted on Aaron to be nice to me. He didn't know that I just wanted to get fucked, as quickly as I could. Gayl could've had adnexitis, I read – inflammation of the Fallopian tubes, the uterus, the ovaries too.

'Wils is in love with someone, Myra, someone you know and fucking like! Okay. Hang on, I'll put you on speaker so you can ask him yourself.'

Aaron took another long bubble hit. I heard Wils say, 'Be careful, man.'

'Wils, please tell Myra what it is that you love most about our lady Lee.'

'She's not who you think she is,' I said before Wils could talk. I don't know why I said that. I was conscious that it wasn't right, that it was betrayal. But I felt it inside me: I had to fuck something up.

'Lee's my partner. It'll be two years in December.'

'I think you don't know everything about her.'

'What the fuck is she talking about, Aar?'

'Hey, hey! Myra's cool. What's going on, Myra, are you being, like, psychic or something?'

'What does that mean?' Wils said.

'It means that she's smart, like, her body is an instrument.'

I was surprised that Aaron said that, considering what was going on, I mean, what I wanted from him. Nothing physical had happened with us in a while.

'Maybe Myra will help you with Lee,' I heard Aaron say.

'Lee's elusive,' Wils said. 'And I don't need any help.'

'So how's your sex?' I asked.

'Don't be so crude, Myra, Jesus!' Wils shouted. A truck honked. 'Aaron, slow the fuck down!'

'You've made her come?'

'Fuck you.'

'Is she good?'

'Yeah, she's intense … '

Then I heard Wils take a toke, the babbling brook. 'Why should I tell you anything, Myra?'

'Because I'm curious. Because I'm brilliant.'

Aaron said something that I couldn't hear. Wils laughed.

'I believe you,' he said.

Now I was in the car too.

'Um, okay. Lee breathes all over me really fast, she gets in my ear and I feel kind of smothered by her,' Wils started. 'Then, listen, at night, when she's sleeping, she can't really breathe. She has some kind of problem with breathing. She loses her breath, or it's like she holds each breath in and she makes this weird sound when it's coming out as if she's deciding if she should take another breath. It's kind of a whining sound, like a crack in the floorboards.'

'Sounds spiritual,' I said. 'Like she's dreaming about breathing.'

'Maybe you're right,' Wils said.

'Maybe she just really needs to explode.'

'Shut the fuck up, Myra. Do you ever shut up?'

'Fuck you too, Wils.'

'Bad blood between you kids, or what?' Aaron laughed.

'Myra thinks she's, like, the greatest lay in the world.'

Maybe Lee had told Wils about me and Elijah.

'Easy. Myra's just curious, you know.'

'She's *not* curious, Aaron. She just doesn't know what the fuck she wants so she's going to fuck over *everyone*.'

'That true, Myra?' Aaron said. 'You wanna fuck me over or just fuck?'

It was true that I was going to be the greatest lay in the world. I was going to experience so much that everyone would want me. I'd be a master and a slave. Elijah and Gayl would take me back.

'What d'you think, My?' Aaron was so stoned.

'I'll wait up for you,' I said.

GAYL: Thank the Lord below. Amen. Myra's going to get laid. Maybe now some shit will change.

§

My mother called from Seoul for the first time since she'd left. The line was so bad that I heard my voice echo first.

'Myra! Oh shit! I just realized it's the middle of the night. I was just about to hang up … I forgot your birthday, Myra, I'm so sorry, my god, I can't believe I did that, please forgive me.'

My mother sounded squealish. Maybe that was the distance.

'Myra, you there? Yes? Oh god, I'm just so glad you picked up. You're awake! I was going to hang up. Oh, Myra, I'm so sorry about your birthday, it's upside-down here. I really miss you. I miss you all.'

'Okay.'

'I've just been getting everything together, you know, my documents, a bank account, all my stuff and getting jobs, teaching jobs, I mean, I can't believe it's been almost a month. Everything takes so long here. It's just such a *thing* being over here, it's like your life is upside-down! I mean, that's not quite right, I mean that I feel upside-down. I feel like I'm standing on my head.'

'You could've called. You could've emailed, right? It would've taken one second.'

'Myra, I *know*. God, I'm sorry. I miss you guys. I miss you and Jody and Jeff so much. I question myself all the time if this was the right thing. I'm sorry, I promised myself I wasn't going to talk about this and blame myself. But you're right, I should've called. You're seventeen.'

'So where are you staying? Can I call you?'

'Oh god! That's funny. My cell is only Asian right now. I'm living at this place called a love hotel, can you believe that? And there's only a communal phone, or something like that. I'm going to get my cell to be international sometimes, I just haven't figured out hardly anything here, it's crazy, and Jon and Sarah left, they went to Japan! They decided they didn't like Seoul or something, when it's so incredible, I mean it, I think you'd like it. Oh, Myra ... '

'What's a love hotel?'

'Sorry, I'm rambling, right? I know I am. But, anyway, most kids here live with their parents until they're married, practically, it's an economic reality. So, most apartments are pretty small here and the kids have to go somewhere to be together, you know, and have sex.'

'And you're living in there?'

'I am. It's really a nice place. I have my own bathroom.'

'Do you hear the kids doing it?'

'Oh god. It's not like that, Myra. I mean, it's like a rooming house, a little hotel, and oh, it's not just kids, anyway … Oh, whatever. I guess most people living here are English teachers like me.'

'You like those people?'

'Who?'

'The people at the motel.'

'Sure I do, I've met some really great kids. I mean, not kids, they're younger than me but they're not kids. They can't believe I have teenagers, actually! They think I'm younger than I am.' My mother started laughing. She didn't hear my echo. 'Myra? You there? Oh, the line's bad. There's people from all over the world here. It's been very inspiring for me.'

'There's people from Africa there?'

'Yes, actually, funny you mention. There's a guy from Nigeria on the floor above me. Oh, the Korean women are just beautiful, it's a really beautiful, beautiful city, Myra, and I'm going to travel around a bit too.'

Now I started laughing. I didn't know why except that I hurt.

'You sound good, Myra, it's so good to hear your voice,' my mom said. She was so far away. 'You know, I think that Nigerian man is in the arms trade or something … '

There was a long patch of static and my mom was laughing through it.

'This line's going to die soon, I'm sorry.'

'Okay.'

'Ummmm … How's your cheek doing now? Is Dr. Bernhard still taking care of it?'

I heard my mother breathing through the receiver. It occurred to me how funny it was, how perfect it was that porn likes a red cheek and a good spanking slap.

'My cheek is perfect,' I said.

'Oh, I'm glad, Myra … How is your dad? I mean, how's he doing?'

'I'm not going to tell you about him.'

'Oh … '

'We're fine, all right? Everything's perfectly fine.'

'I'll call Jeff tomorrow. Jody's really loving residence, she says. And she says that you're seeing someone? I mean, that you've been spending time with someone?'

Fucking god. I *knew* whatever Lee said to my dad would travel fast. I had no idea if Lee had told my father about Elijah, or Aaron. If Lee was as bad now as Jen and Charlene.

'Dad is a troll.'

My mom said nothing.

I went on in the void, through our dying line. 'He sleeps in the basement and comes home from work early and then he's on his computer all night. What do you think he's doing down there?'

'His problems are not your problems, okay?'

'I still live here, right? You don't. So you don't know.'

'I don't want to hear about you babying your dad! He's an adult, for god's sake. I want to hear about you.'

'I'm not babying him! He gives me and Jeff twenty bucks a week to get us out of the house and shut us up.'

'I'm sending you guys money soon. Please. You don't have to worry about your father. It's disgusting … '

'It's not disgusting.'

'Myra, I have to get off the phone, there's someone waiting.'

'Fine. Go.'

'I'll come back, you know.' My mother's voice was a pipsqueak.

'No you won't.'

'I will.'

'Well, I won't need you anymore when you do.'

§

Aaron staggered into my bedroom around five in the morning. He was jumping on one foot like a monkey in the rain. I shut the door tight.

'It smells like Indian food in here, My.'

Aaron slid off his shirt and jeans. His chest was bony, the colour of a peach. His cock looked like a rag that he squeezed and let go.

'I got here as fast as I could. I'm sorry, I'm just so fucking horny for you.'

Now his penis was a wire. He was searching on the floor in the pockets of his jeans. I watched him slide a condom on himself.

'You're so fucking sexy, Myra.'

I wasn't doing anything. I was just standing there watching him, feeling cold.

'Wils was laughing at me how fast I ditched him. Come on, you need help?'

I didn't need help. I unzipped my jeans. I felt my hands under my armpits and I took off my T-shirt. Inside my head was Elijah, just Elijah. They made me leave them. My nipples were hard. I wanted to be at Filmore's, my love hotel.

'Oh man, I love your body, your breasts, I love all your hair.'

I shuffled over to Aaron who was now lying flat on my bed, just his cock standing up. I stretched my legs and climbed over him. Aaron kept closing his eyes and opening them. His lids were purple-red like his cock. It looked like he was falling asleep. But he was so hard. He was reaching up for me and I just did it. Easy. I climbed right on. Climbed on and slid down. Aaron yelped. My thighs swung out to each side in a squat. I felt like an orangutan. It didn't even hurt. The flute hurt. I was good for a second when Aaron held my waist and started rocking me around. I got into it and I closed my eyes and kind of danced and bounced on top of him. I put my hands on the wall over his head. Aaron was rocking into me pretty hard when suddenly he sat up like an ironing board, one of those ones just popped out of a wall. He buried his head in my tits and jerked up so hard that my bed moved a foot away from the wall.

'I'm gonna come,' he said. 'Is it okay if I come?'

'Yes.'

I held on as his body got tiny and iron, he grunted and sweated but his sweat had turned cold. Aaron was licking me, kissing and biting my neck as he fell out of me, saying, 'Oh fucking, man, Myra. Thank you so much.'

I scissored up off him. His penis was a dot.

I thought about Lee, I thought about my mother. I didn't want to be in some silent game of female mistrust.

§

I started my essay with the line *You could be raped a thousand times and you could still be a virgin.*

This was also my thesis, the force behind every word about the freedom of slaves.

It occurred to me that my mother was reading that book on the comfort women of Korea because she'd been planning to go there for a while. The comfort women in the Second World War are grandmothers now and they are asking the Korean and the Japanese governments, 'Is it right to ignore me like this as if they did nothing to me? Were the soldiers justified in trampling an innocent and fragile teenage girl and making her suffer for the rest of her life?' The Korean comfort women have stopped covering their faces at their public gatherings. They have realized, forty years later, that they were not dirty, that they had done nothing wrong.

§

When I knocked on their door I was not a virgin anymore. Gayl answered in a tight pink dress with embroidery on it, a spiral, fuchsia, over her chest.

'Where in the hell did you go for so long?'

'What do you mean?'

Gayl ushered me in. 'See? He wants to be with you. Look at that sorry dog.'

'Fuff! Fuff fuff!' Elijah was in bed. He barked under the sheets.

'It's not fuff, it's *ruff*,' I said, kind of surprised. 'Like: RUFFF RUFF RUFFF!'

Elijah and Gayl laughed at my impression.

'We got a wildebeest there.' Elijah crawled out of the sheets.

'Yeah, yeah, a dangerous one.'

'*De bitch of de north.*'

'All newly laid.'

I stared at Gayl. She winked. She knew. How the fuck did she know? Gayl took me by the hand. Her hand was warm. She seemed all better and strong. Adnexitis happened after miscarriage, I'd read. It caused infertility. It was a violation of sexual function.

Gayl turned on the TV to the country-music station. There was a skinny blond woman on there singing in a headdress. Gayl swung me around the room in a square dance or something. Her arms were so strong that I was lifting off the floor. Elijah clapped along to the beat.

'Make your mountains higher, make 'em higher each day,' the woman sang on TV. 'Make it so your sunshine is brighter than a ray.'

Then the blonde took a bow and her headdress fell off. Elijah clapped. Gayl gave me a hard little quick little hug.

'Seriously, why'd you leave us alone here? We don't really know this town and you make him feel so much better. Look at him. See how he feels better?'

Elijah was naked. His cock was straight up. He was holding it at the bottom with two hands, like a shovel. It was pointing at me. I was breathing hard.

'Don't leave us anymore, Myra. You understand?'

It felt good to hear her say my name. I was buzzing from my feet to my hair. I felt like Gayl was going to be my friend. She supported my union with Elijah, not Lee.

GAYL: See? You see how I got her converted?
LEE: Your tactics are suspect. I don't like that at all.

GAYL: *She's* the wormy little suspect, your friend. I'll give her back when I'm finished. Natch.

LEE: Bitch.

GAYL: You like it like that.

§

My dad was taking Jeff to his overnight hockey tournament. I was making dinner for Elijah. I had an old recipe book of my mom's, a yellow binder with quick leek quiche and spaghetti and meatballs, all these family standards. My mother's writing marked up the margins: *Neil likes onions. Jeff finds carrots too hard. Jody and Myra eat broccoli in this.*

I decided to make the whole dinner the day before: unpacking the meat, frying garlic, two onions, boiling in a couple of cans of skinned-out tomatoes, a cinnamon stick, bay leaf, five peppercorns. *Add one cup of wine. Less, if the kids.* When I measured the spaghetti for boiling I cooked enough for five – our old number around the table. But my mom and Jody had fled the coop. Dad and Jeff would be gone for the night. I was a lone Hegelian, with a horny pig's tail, a self-conscious slave. I drank our last bottle of burgundy, masturbating, coming ten times in a row.

§

Aaron was drunk, he told me on the phone to warn me. I did not want to see him just because we'd fucked but he basically forced me to see him because he said it wasn't fair that I wouldn't see him, like I'd just *been* with him and how could I not see him after what we did together?

When I got to his room on the third floor, Aaron's eyes were dim grey, like the light had blown out in a bulb. He was laughing at his book, *Gravity and Grace.*

'"Base feelings, envy, resentment are degraded energy,"' Aaron read out loud. 'Come over here, baby. Does anyone call you *baby?*'

He stunk extremely of smoke and beer. Aaron looked up at me so needy that it made me really squirm. He was holding a pipe. He was going to light it.

'I don't think you need that,' I said.

'I'm insatiable, don't you know that?'

I felt sorry for him. Aaron lit the pipe. His cheeks got hollow sucking in. I sat down beside him. He was insatiable for drugs. He wasn't insatiable like I was insatiable. The thing was, he would've been so easily satisfied. I knew I could've done it too, just by kissing him or something. He would've been so happy.

'Why didn't tell me you were with someone else?'

'What do you mean?' It was my first instinct to lie.

'Lee told me.'

Aaron read my silence. He sucked in some more. Fuck. Lee was like Jen and Charlene? Aaron had three paperbacks on the crate beside his mattress. One was called *The Violent Bear it Away*. Flannery O'Connor. Those three books were for me.

'Myra, don't you have anything to say?'

'The violent bear it away.'

Aaron cursed on an exhale. Then he started to whine. 'First, Wils, like, told me about Chris calling you titillating, all right? Next Lee tells me about you and this American dude. Some fucking Rasta? That's just fucked up. It's baffling. I mean, *I* was the first one to find you.'

'Find me?'

'Yeah. It's a fucking *travesty*.'

'What are you talking about?'

Aaron opened a can of beer. He pointed to the one beside it for me. I didn't want it.

'Look. I know you think about fucking all the time.'

He seemed so hurt. I could not speak. It's true that that was what I was thinking about. My essay had evolved into thinking about fucking. You could be raped a thousand times and still be a virgin. I was writing about fucking by a master and fucking as a slave, about Hegel, the comfort women and teenage porno stars. Ms. Bain and Mr. Rotowsky could fail me, I didn't care. I'd pass just with the bibliography. I was compiling a list of every single book I'd read or that I wanted to read that was about power and sex. High school should have a whole fucking course on just this. I was helping the school make curriculum.

Aaron lay on his back on a lumpy stained pillow, holding his beer. 'I'm smarter than you think, Myra. I know you don't wanna sleep with just me. I bet you probably want to sleep with Wils too. It's okay, you're young. I know … '

His eyes couldn't stop closing. I felt sorry for him. I took the can of beer from his hand.

'You're beautiful, Myra. Not titill … titillit … titillating … '

Aaron unzipped his jeans. It took him three tries. His cock moved around inside his shorts. He held it still and closed his eyes. I thought of Elijah on his bed, cock hard and ready, and Gayl leading me away to the bathroom to prepare me. She'd told me that Elijah wasn't ready to fuck me yet but that I should be patient. When it's time, she'd said, it would blow my fucking mind. I moved Aaron's hand. I took his penis out of his shorts and put it in my mouth. I didn't want to but I did.

Aaron was instantly happy, moaning, 'I just want to be your boyfriend, Myra. Myra, let me be your boyfriend.'

I was sucking him but pushing him out. Why wasn't Elijah ready to fuck me? I was prepared! I didn't want a boyfriend. Aaron was inside my mouth and pushing off the mattress and my head now felt like a light bulb too. I was just about to stop when everything inside of him filled up my mouth – everything sour and alive that hated me.

'Sorry, man, sorry, Myra, god.'

It was like he hadn't just come. I wiped my mouth. Aaron helped me do it with the sheet.

'I'm sorry, you didn't know, I'm really sorry, fuck, Myra, you didn't know.'

I didn't want his help with my face. 'I *do* know about that,' I said. Aaron wanted me to be his girlfriend, all romantic and drippy.

'What the fuck?' Aaron's voice went up high.

'Yeah, I'm with someone else,' I said, confirming Lee.

Aaron looked around for the pipe in his sheets. 'So this American Rasta has got a big dick? He shoves it down your throat? You let him cum all over your face? Go on. Tell me all the gory details.'

'Fuck off!' I yelled. 'Why should I tell you about that?'

Aaron was going to cry. 'Lee is a way better girlfriend than you.'

I stood up to leave. Being a girlfriend is a travesty.

LEE: Some guys are not in the space to ever know that a girl they are with has sex without their permission. Guys don't know how to deal with the fact that a girl is free, that she has an autonomous life and an autonomous past and also that the problems in her life aren't meant to be solved. Guys are problem-solvers and girls' problems aren't solvable. Girls' problems *are* their life.

GAYL: Yeah, true, man, I think you're right about that. Myra doesn't even know the meaning of *travesty*.

§

When Elijah came into my bedroom he didn't laugh at all. He picked things up and looked at them closely, like my pillow with the purple silk ruffle and the books I read when I was a kid. Elijah flipped through a folk-tale picture book with stories from around the world. In his scuffed white angel-armed robe he looked like the grand teller of all tales.

'Why's there no Africans in here? We got fairy tales too.'

Elijah stopped at Little Red Riding Hood from France. I remembered that story really well, my mother read it to me every night for a while when I was seven. In that French version, the wolf kills the grandmother and he makes Little Red Riding Hood drink her grandmother's blood from a bottle. The wolf gets so close then to getting Little Red Riding Hood in the bed but she escapes, I remembered, by saying she had to pee. The wolf was suspicious so he tied Little Red Riding Hood's ankle with a rope so that she could pee outside and he didn't have to get out of bed but he knew that he still had her. Me and my mother liked that part. We called the wolf 'jailer lazy.' So of course Little Red Riding Hood tricks the wolf – she takes the rope off her ankle and ties it to a tree so that the wolf just thinks she's peeing for a really long time. But when he pulls the rope, he can't get her back. Little Red Riding Hood escapes home to her mom.

It was three o'clock in the afternoon. My father and Jeff were supposed to come home late at night. There was time for a few things to happen.

I felt brave when Elijah was in my room. 'I only know a little bit about you,' I said, happy that I had him here, that Gayl was out of the equation. 'I want to know more about you, I mean.'

Elijah sat down on my single mattress still looking at Little Red Riding Hood. He seemed oversize in here. He wanted to talk, not kiss. And not fuck fuck fuck.

'We were working on the way up north,' he said. 'Tobacco farm, other stuff, the dregs. It's why we took so long to get to you.'

'A tobacco farm? Why?'

Elijah showed me his hands. There were four oval calluses along the top line of his palms. Faith, who used to clean our house, I remembered that she had calluses there too.

'We hear there's more work up in Brantford, near here.'

'You're going to leave?'

'We're on a path of work,' Elijah said. 'And Brantford is only an hour from here.'

'Oh.'

Elijah put down my book of fairy tales. 'What's wrong, Angel?'

'I mean … who's Gayl, then? I mean, really, to you?'

'You're trying to figure her out now? You're smart, aren't you?'

I didn't know what to say. I'm not smart when it comes to you, I wanted to say. I would be smart if you fucked me! Please fuck me and I'll know everything I need to.

But Elijah got up from my bed and walked out of my bedroom where I thought we would've done something. I followed him through my own house. He looked at Jody's old room first, reached under her pillow and opened her closet. All she had in there were stacks of old shoes, boots and clothes. Then Elijah skipped across the hall into my parents' room, straight into their walk-in closet. He noticed that the side where my mom's clothes were supposed to be was empty. There was just one thing hanging, a white off-the-shoulder dress, something she hadn't worn in years. Elijah didn't poke much around in Jeff's baby-blue room with all the posters of anime. He walked back down the hallway, then down the stairs. In the kitchen he looked in our fridge full of takeout containers. My pan of pre-stirred, pre-made spaghetti bolognese had thick yellow spots congealed on the top. Elijah grabbed a couple of old purple grapes that were rolling around on the bottom of the fruit drawer. He didn't wash them before he popped them in his mouth.

'These are anti-estrogen,' Elijah said. 'Not like that flesh.'

I felt too embarrassed to say something. It didn't even occur to me that Elijah was a vegetarian but now the robes he wore made a bit more sense. Rastafarians are vegetarians, I was sure Jody knew that.

'Animal is bad for you,' Elijah said, as he flicked my boob through my shirt.

Even that crappy flick made my nipples hard.

I followed Elijah down to the basement, my father's lair. I hadn't been down there since my mother left. My dad had strung makeshift curtains around a mattress on the floor. Inside the hut was his computer too, on a cheap brown desk.

'I like this,' Elijah said. 'Privacy. Men need that.'

Elijah turned on my father's computer from a switch at the back. It smelled like my dad inside these curtains, but sharper, like the inside of a boot. I had no idea why he'd walled himself off in a fort but it felt kind of creepy being inside it. Elijah didn't look at me as he waited for the computer. He sat down on my dad's swirly brown chair and spun around in it a bunch of times. It was really weird now to have him here. I didn't feel brave at all anymore. Elijah hadn't wanted to stay in my bedroom. He wanted to be in my father's chair.

I think it would have been my mother, though, not my father, who'd be the most shocked at this scene: an older man, a Rastafarian vegetarian in a white angel robe, MYRA'S LOVER, twirling around in Neil's curtain-walled, stinky, unnatural fort.

Elijah was pulling up a bunch of files. He seemed to know what he was doing.

'Don't do that!' I said. 'It's my dad's stuff.'

'Your daddy watches *Girls Gone Wild*?'

'Don't,' I said again, going closer to the screen. I was getting worried about Elijah fucking up all the programs.

'Looky look,' Elijah laughed.

A photo came up on the screen full-size: it was a twenty-year-old girl in a bright pink string bikini who was using one red-nailed finger to pull the elastic away from her thigh. Elijah clicked. Another photo came up of that girl with the red-nailed finger inside herself. Her teeth were ridged. There was this blurry naked guy in the background holding a beer.

'Cum shot,' Elijah said, talking to the screen. 'Fuck her. Fuck her.'

'What is that?' I said.

I knew what it was. My fucking computer upstairs was overrun with it too.

'Your family photos?'

Elijah laughed again. I didn't believe that my father was looking at this. Elijah kept clicking, there were thousands of pictures and videos too of college girls in bikinis rubbing oil on their tits. I remembered that porn in Key West, my very first porn. Oh god, my father. I was going to throw up. Me in his fort and our porn was a revolting kind of link.

'I can find Gayl on here too,' Elijah said.

But now a blond girl in a bright pink bikini danced with her top hanging off and her fingers digging up in another twenty-year-old's bikini. Their tits were touching, they were rubbing and giggling.

Sweat prickled under my arms. Elijah twisted around in my dad's swirly chair and got me to sit on the edge of his knee. Our basement had walls that looked like wood.

'Who are these girls, is this all from the States?' I don't know why I pretended I didn't know about porn.

'Yeah, Angel. Key West, maybe.'

Is that why we could find Gayl in the porn?

Elijah pulled one of my hands behind me and stuck it on his crotch. His cock was bulging under his robe. With my arm twisted back, the videos kept playing. Bikini tops off, the bottoms off too. I could see inside the girls, they were parting themselves. I felt myself slipping off Elijah's knee. Those girls didn't have any hair on their vaginas. I was happy when I started growing hair down there.

Elijah whispered in my ear: 'Someone in this house has a very dirty mind.'

I didn't know why the video was making me horny. It was fucking disgusting. It was my *dad's*. I felt like Elijah was going to fuck me right then. I was totally queasy, horny and queasy. Elijah put his hand on my tit over my shirt and he was squeezing and pinching my nipple with one hand and using his other hand on the mouse. We swivelled in a semicircle closer to the screen.

Then someone walked into the screen and I whipped my head away.

'Come on, come on,' Elijah laughed. With his forehead, he butted me back.

In the video it looked like my father. My father taking off his pants over the girl on the floor. It looked just like him, puffy eyes and hairy chin. His moss-and-mould-covered skin, naked and hairy like a troll. There was a man like my father and a girl on her hands and knees. Her pink bikini top hung from her neck.

'I can't,' I said.

'You can. You can.'

There was another older guy in the video now with the man who looked like my dad. I was forced to the screen like eyelid torture. A college girl in some wrung-out bikini with two old guys, one in front of her and one behind. She opened her legs and she opened her mouth. In porn they make fathers screw daughters with other fathers. The girl with the bikini around her neck didn't look sad. She looked like she was going to have an orgasm. I leaned back into Elijah. I was going to vomit.

'You'd like that too? Two guys with you? Huh, you'd like that, Myra, wouldn't you? Gayl would too. But she's better at this shit. She's a real artist.'

I leaned over to the side and hacked. It burnt the back of my throat. Elijah didn't care.

'It's okay that you like it, it's okay you like it, that's okay … '

That's what Lee had said to me too. *It's okay that you want these things to come true.*

Yeah, well, now everything was true. My life was here. And it was friendless and looking at porn with a phantasm of my father, thinking of Gayl the Artist on a cock-hard lap.

§

I was writing my essay, writing easily now. I didn't have a reader anymore like Lee or Chris but I imagined that I was writing for them both. Maybe I was writing for anyone who could fucking stand me. I'd changed my title to *The Pornography Liberation Narrative and Sex Slaves: A Synthesis.*

'Pornography is exhilarating and revolting simultaneously,' I wrote, thinking of my father's stash of porn that had morphed at the end into Rent-A-Maid sites. 'Pornography links up the internal, the external and the fantastical ways that we are not yet in the world with the ways that we might very well be.'

Me and Elijah made out that night with the porno sounds on. He wanted me to start at his feet. I kissed his toes and travelled up under his robe to his big-eyed, big thick, all-seeing cock. I sucked him off under there the best that I had ever done it. Elijah moaned *goddamn, fucking Christ, shit, my lord.*

'Pornography shows us things that are only at the edges of our imagination,' I wrote. 'Pornography shoves this edge at us violently.'

Before he left our house that night, Elijah told me something that I replayed and replayed, the way Lee did when her teacher told her how hot her body was. 'Myra, you are my favourite little actress,' Elijah said. 'It's your little hands, you're so greedy, you grab at me. You really want me, don't you?'

Yeah, yeah, I do! I am your *favourite*.

'I like that it's no act, my hot little actress.'

I was an *actress*, his favourite hot greedy little actress!

'Pornography is a mirror of us, a mirror of our self-consciousness,' I wrote, 'our master self-consciousness and our slave self-consciousness that comes together and rips into the way we were born. Pornography is the liberation narrative that takes us out of the family pen. It synthesizes the secret and the domestic, the explicit and the implicit, the master and the slave. This is a synthesis that we must absorb in our lives.'

Elijah likes me. I'm his favourite. I desperately had to tell the whole world.

'In literature,' I wrote, 'synthesis is a technique of open interpretation or postmodern analysis, wherein we analyze a text from a multiplicity of viewpoints. In history, this is called Dialectics. Hegel said that history is a dialectic, a constant struggle between factions. Pornography and the innocence of it is a mode of learning, a constant struggle, that synthesizes our understanding of the opposites within ourselves.'

I was an actress not acting. A being *being*.

§

Wils set me up another big hit from the bong. Aaron looked angry and I knew he hadn't wanted to see me. 'You're driving me to alcoholism,' he'd said on the phone. 'I'm a pacifist pothead and you're driving me to drink.'

But I needed to see them, I was lonely. It was 4 a.m. Lee wasn't there, apparently she'd just left, and our silence continued.

'I always wanted to be the prettiest person in a room,' I began my story to Aaron and Wils, feeling desperate for their attention, like a runaway. Lee was prettier than me. She was a better girlfriend. 'Or I always wanted to look like other girls, someone else, not myself, there was always someone who looked better and more beautiful than me.'

Aaron took a swig of rum. 'I think you're the most beautiful girl I've ever seen,' he said.

'Once in Grade 8, listen to this, you guys: I slapped my best friend Jen across the face. She was the most popular, most good-looking girl in the school. I slapped her because she was laughing hysterically. She'd started laughing so hard at her own story about some guy, I don't even remember what the story was, and her laughs became yaps, like hysterical air-swallowing. I just wanted her to shut up so badly that I slapped her. Her ponytail swung from side to side but even that didn't stop her yapping for a second. You get what happened? I mean, right after I smacked her? She started *really* laughing after I slapped her cheek. My slapping had actually made things worse. I mean, she couldn't stop that terrible laughing-crying-yapping for another ten minutes!'

Wils was smiling at my story but Aaron was grim.

'It felt good to slap her,' I said. 'To slap the most beautiful girl to attempt to stop her self-destruction ... '

'Yeah, Myra? What'd she think? Did she like it too?'

I ignored Aaron's spite. 'We didn't talk about it afterwards, I mean, after she finally calmed down. She was shocked, I think, but she wasn't mad. Jen held her cheek and there were tears on her face, but she couldn't stop staring at me in total relief. It was like she knew that she needed it. Maybe if she'd said anything afterwards it would've just been *thank you. Thank you for slapping me into myself.* Me and Jen were best friends for four years after that.'

'That's it,' Wils said slowly. 'That's totally it. People don't really know what other people need anymore.'

Aaron got up to go to the bathroom.

Smoke hovered in the room between me and Wils. I did not miss being friends with Jen.

I lay down on Aaron's lumpy pillow and I looked up at Wils. 'See, I guess Gayl knew what I needed when she slapped me.'

When Gayl slapped me, she shocked me out of a dream, my old way of thinking. My needs were bigger than my family's needs. I needed Gayl, I needed her slap to crack out of my world.

Aaron staggered back into the room. Wils stood up to block him because both of us saw he was suddenly rabid. 'I can't take this, man, I can't take her anymore. I can't take your stories. I don't want to see your face. Get the fuck out of here! You're driving me to the abyss, Myra. Can you leave, man? Now. Jesus. I can't see you ever again, I can't see her for a while ... '

Aaron's two black eyes were fixated on me.

'I think you should go,' Wils whispered at me. He had his arm around Aaron, holding him up.

'Yeah, go live your life or something. Go fuck a pole. You're fucking me up.'

Aaron leaned his head on Wils' shoulder. He took his book, his coverless bible – Weil's *Gravity and Grace* – and whipped it across the room at me. The book hit the wall. Aaron closed his eyes. Wils was whispering to him.

I picked up the book and I left the room like the lone fucking wolf with a Bible in its teeth. I was off to tie Little Red Riding Hood to a tree.

LEE: Watch her run, watch her run through the woods.

GAYL: Yeah, watch, we're getting climactic.

§

By the time I got to Filmore's, I was stoned in a bubble of Weil. 'A test of what is real is that it is hard and rough. Joys are found in it, not pleasure. What is pleasant belongs to dreams.'

The pages were falling out of the book. I folded loose pages between other pages.

The door of their room was half-open. Gayl slept twisted up in her sheets. The other bed was empty. Quietly, I went to the bathroom. Elijah was there under fluorescent lights, eyes closed, his beard a maze of tiny black chains. His robe was half-off. His chest was a bull's chest, slick with sweat. I felt dizzy at the doorway, like I should just leave. I didn't know why he was sitting in there. Was he waiting for me? Elijah shivered and he opened his eyes.

'I miss you when you're with your family,' he said.

He'd been waiting for me. 'I miss you too,' I said. I wanted to sit on his lap.

'I missed you, Angel, from two thousand miles away.'

I felt a sluggish pulse in my throat and between my legs, the same slow throbs. It made me think I was in love. Me and Elijah were strangers in love. Maybe love like ours could be eternal.

'Stay with us now,' Elijah said. 'Just stay.'

I didn't need to ask him what I should do, or wait for anything anymore. I knew what to do and I knew what I wanted.

I knew what he meant when he said *us*.

I took off my underwear from under my skirt. My limbs felt swollen, twice their size. Elijah stared at my skirt, under where I was hairy. I felt joy, not pleasure. This was real, not a dream. The lights were on. I wanted to keep the lights on. I looked over in the mirror as Elijah slid his hands up my T-shirt. I saw the door open a crack. She was there, Gayl the Artist, with a video camera, clear black and glass.

As I straddled Elijah I got out of my bra but kept on my shirt. My purse was still on, the strap sucked tight to my chest.

'I'm your slave,' I whispered. 'I'll stay if you let me be your slave.'

Gayl was filming us through the crack in the door.

'Take this off too,' Elijah said, pulling my T-shirt away from my breasts.

'No,' I said. 'It looks better with it on.'

I would be a collaborator. I would be the artist's collaborator in my own porn.

Elijah started squeezing my breasts and moving them around. His face looked suddenly rocky, disturbed. Was this their plan the whole time? From Key West? To be their hot little actress? I placed my hands on the scummy tiles above Elijah's head. I was scared for one second about my mother and my father, that they were going to find out what I was doing.

Gayl entered the bathroom. The video camera covered half of her face. Two braids touched her shoulders, her hair was unwound. I looked back at her and I tried to wink but I laughed instead. I saw a part of her mouth opening, the apple in her cheek. The video camera made the sound of a fan.

Elijah moved his robe to one side. His cock stood straight up.

'She's never done it before,' Elijah said seriously, staring at Gayl's camera. 'She's my horny little virgin slave.'

Elijah opened a drawer under the sink. There were three open boxes of rubbers in there. Elijah ripped open the corner of one with his teeth.

I was going to make people come without touching themselves.

The condom looked like it had saliva on it. Elijah played with the tip of it before rolling it over himself.

Somehow, right then, I knew the whole script. I knew the whole script of virginity.

'I'm gonna be this girl's first.'

I was ready to make-believe. Elijah looked at Gayl, right into the camera: 'Don't you want to be this girl's first and break her cherry fucking hard?'

'Yeah, an innocent virgin,' Gayl finally spoke. 'An innocent slut with an incredible body. Spread her thighs a little wider for the shot.'

'Like this?' I asked.

'Yeah, that looks good. You can almost see her hymen stretch.'

I started to laugh.

'See? Virgins love to fuck!'

Elijah had my waist hard and was guiding me down. I lowered myself, holding strong in my thighs. I squeezed my eyes shut. I knew how I looked.

'Wait, slave. Open your eyes.'

I couldn't open my eyes. Gayl was so close behind me I felt her breath on my back.

'Fine, I got it. Go on, push her down. Hey, slave: open your eyes.'

I opened my eyes. A sharp pain ran through me. I gave myself all the way on Elijah. It hurt. It felt good. It didn't hurt to feel good. I felt buzzing now in me. It was magical. The camera pinged. Elijah leaned all the way back to the wall so the crown of his head was touching the tiles. My hands held the sides of his arms and I bounced up and down. His neck was like mink. I moved around in a circle to try to feel even more.

'She's a natural, see how horny virgins are?'

Gayl liked what I was doing. Her voice was hoarse.

'Look over here, slave. Let your lips open. Show me your tongue.'

I was their slave. My lips were ringed with lipstick and spit.

'She's the best, G., let's only use her from now on.'

'I knew she'd be. She's my favourite. I told her.'

I licked Elijah's neck. I felt the smallest centre line of my body divide.

This was a true loss of virginity: a multiplication of joy from a division of my self.

'Look over here again, slave, show me your tits.'

I was trying to look over at Gayl, the black glass eye in front of her face. But Elijah pinched my waist and started forcing me up and down like a doll so hard that I thought he was going to make me fall off. Elijah looked like he was running on the spot. Gayl hovered on top of us.

Elijah shook his head side to side and he grunted up hard. I felt his cock twitch. I stood up too quickly. He tried to shove me back down on him but my knees were already locked straight. The condom slipped off him. I was wet. I wanted the floor. I wasn't laughing anymore. I heard all our breaths flying out in the room.

Gayl pointed her camera down. She was filming me crouched down on the floor. I held on to Elijah's legs. I covered myself.

'Hold yourself open.'

I knew I could make myself come without touching myself.

'C'mon, slave, you can do it.'

Gayl's camera was a beast with the tail hanging down.

'Yeah, like that, that looks good. Tell us how it feels not to be a virgin anymore.'

I couldn't answer. I was a being *being*.

'God, you're amazing,' Gayl went on. She was watching me, my chest up and down, my legs all relaxed. My throat and my cunt in one suctioned tube. I was making myself cum without touching myself. I looked at Gayl through her beast-like eye. 'This is the best I've ever seen, Elijah. She's ecstatic, my lord. Come on, slave, tell us, tell us how your first fucking feels.'

The condom glistened in Elijah's cupped, callused hand. He held it like a crystal. I squeezed inside myself until I came, no hands, no thoughts, a great gush on the floor.

'That's how it feels,' I got out, catching my breath. 'I came all over your fucking place.'

Gayl didn't turn off the camera, Elijah didn't move from his seat. I found my clothes on the floor and got dressed.

My pussy felt bloated, it smiled and glared.

I walked to the subway in the weak morning sun. I let people look at my freshly fucked and filmed face. My head was high like royalty. I felt tender too. The kind of tenderness that could kill someone.

I'd just been in a magical porn. It was the climax of my self-fucking-worth.

✘ ✘ ✘

Maidenhead

I made sure the side door didn't click. In the glare of the kitchen was the head of my father on the table, my mom's yellow recipe book as his pillow.

'Why were you so late?' The head roused, eyes small.

'I was out with Lee and Aaron at a party.'

'No.'

'I was.'

'I spoke to Lee last night.'

The sun shone on my father's face.

'She says you two haven't spoken in a week.'

I tried to move past him. I wasn't even surprised. I was pissed. 'You know I've heard all this before, right? The worried friends … '

'This time *I'm* worried.'

'Yeah?'

'Who is this man that even Jen told me about, for chrissake?'

'Dad … '

'No. You just can't be with a man who is so much older than you.'

I laughed. 'Why not?'

'It's dangerous.'

'Yeah? And what's wrong with danger?' I felt like I was talking to my mother.

My father stood up. 'I will not allow you to be in danger.'

'Come on. That's funny.'

'It is not funny!'

'Oh god. Dad. I'm not in danger, okay?' I have a cock around my neck as a talisman against violence.

'Where is this man staying?'

'Downtown.'

'Where. I asked *where*.'

I was quiet. The sun disappeared.

'You know, if you want to know so much about *this man*, just chat with Lee again. I'm fine with that, actually. She's such a great storyteller. A great listener too. So just go huddle with her, okay?'

I finally got past my father. He was guilty and tight.

He cleared his throat strangely. 'We have a cleaning lady coming here today,' he said. 'She was here last week too. She's been a few times. Her name is Anna.'

'Fine. Do I need to clean my room?'

'No! She's going to do it.'

'I don't want her in my room.'

'Anna is from Indonesia.'

'Great.'

I ran upstairs and slammed my door; left him stuck in the sun with that book of my mom's.

LEE: I miss that fucked-up sneak.

GAYL: I still have her.

LEE: I'll have her back soon.

GAYL: Sabotage!

LEE: Reality.

GAYL: Myra's learning, finally, what is real.

§

When I arrived that night at Filmore's, I was a brand-new woman. Gayl was gone. So was the sack where she kept her camera and cords. Elijah said that she needed some air.

'She's suspicious,' he said. He went back to his bed, crawled under the covers.

Now that I finally knew what they did together, I didn't believe him. I mean, what the fuck was she suspicious about? Gayl and Elijah made porn. And I was a porn connoisseur. I was a porn scholar! I was there to tell Elijah that I wanted to do it again. I wanted to be filmed. I wanted to hear Gayl and Elijah talk about me while we fucked. I loved that part, when Gayl said, *She's the best one we've ever had*. I wanted to be a porn star. I wanted to move to L.A. and get a website or something. Gayl could be my manager. There were girls like me. I knew there were girls out there like me. Girls who liked to be in porn. Girls who liked to make men feel. We would all be together, me, her and him. I was changing up my life, climbing out of the hole of not knowing who I was. I could be anything 'cause I had porn in my blood!

Elijah looked towards the door. 'Well, look who's finally found her way back.'

I hoped that Gayl had her camera and was ready for something. But the lock was stuck, she started banging against the door. I ran over to open it for her.

'Holy fuck! What happened to you?'

Gayl had two black eyes and a puffed-up mouth.

She pushed by me to Elijah in the bed. His arms opened and she curled up on his body like a cat.

'I'll get ice!' I said.

The hallway stunk of smoke and beer. Ice would bring that swelling down. My mother put ice on my face in the bathtub in Key West.

Gayl was crying and whispering to Elijah when I came back in with the bucket. She was in these tight black jeans with a short white leather jacket that showed her stomach. I'd never seen her so done up.

It didn't occur to me then, holding the ice and watching her squirm on his lap, that he might have been the one who did that to her.

'I don't want that,' Gayl said to me, her face in Elijah's chest.

I put the ice bucket down on the floor.

'I don't like you, Myra,' Gayl said. She kissed Elijah's beard. She got up off his lap and lay down on the floor. She pulled her camera bag out from deep under the bed. Her lip was bleeding. 'I think you look good on a screen, but I don't like you.'

Gayl passed Elijah the video camera.

'Why do you have to be so mean to me?'

Elijah started laughing. I knew I sounded like Jen, spoiled and naive: *Why don't you like me? Why do you have to be so mean?*

I couldn't conclude my essay. I couldn't bring it all together. I didn't know how getting fucked a thousand times turned a slave free in Hegel's dialectic.

It took me a second to realize that Elijah was filming, that Gayl was shimmying, puffy-eyed, towards me. Even barefoot, she was so much taller than me. I looked back at Elijah. The big black glass eye in front of his face. There are slaves on the earth right now. Gayl took off her white leather jacket.

'Ready, E.? You ready for the first take?'

'What is going on, you guys?'

Gayl slapped me across the head. Elijah shot it. I reached my hand up but she hit my other side hard.

'Stop!' I screamed.

Gayl didn't stop. She looked back at Elijah and he circled in closer, climbing up on the bed. Gayl slapped my head for a third and fourth time.

'I don't like this,' I was yelling. 'Turn off that thing!'

'It's okay, Angel. Tell her, Gayl.'

Gayl concentrated. She didn't speak. She was concentrating on performing, on pummelling me. I didn't know why it was happening and I never stopped screaming, trying to grab at her hand before it smacked down.

'Turn that off! Or I'm going to kill you!'

Gayl danced lighter on her feet. 'Man, this is good. *She's* going to kill *me*.'

Finally, I thought of something right to protect myself. I crouched down near the skirts of the bed, slid on my belly and hid my head in my arms. She couldn't slap me like that. But Gayl kicked my sides in with her bare feet.

'You getting this, 'Jah?'

Elijah grunted from up high.

'Stop, please just stop it!'

'You're a little fucking baby who has been pampered all her life.'

Spit rained down on the back of my neck. She was winning the fight. It wasn't a fight.

'You listen to me, listen to this.'

'Look up,' Elijah ordered.

I would not look up. I would not fucking look up if they were going to do this to me. Slaves revolt. I remembered this.

'Myra? Hey, Myra?'

I didn't look up and the beating stopped.

'Angel?'

'Actress?'

'Our beautiful bitch?'

Breathing, I slowly showed them an eye. Elijah hung over the edge of the bed with the camera. Gayl was a half-naked totem pole above me.

'You've been living in a world of privilege and it's made you crazy,' Gayl said softly. 'Look at her eye. Look at that innocent eye. You're useless right now, baby. You need to grow up. You took a vacation on the backs of slaves. You and your family having fun like that. That is crazy. It is criminal. Stand up now. You can do it. Come on, stand up, baby. You're strong, come on. You're hurt, okay, but get up. Get this, Elijah. Come on, get her right now.'

I decided to obey. It would be easiest to obey her at this moment. It would be most useful to obey.

I felt my hands on the floor. I pushed up, then I stood there, exposed. Pounding rotated near my eyes. The camera beeped. Gayl was swaying, tall. Her fingers crunched and turned into a fist. The camera flashed. Gayl punched me in the jaw.

Oh god, Lee, please tell my father that I'm here! My family didn't have fun on our vacation! My family split up on that vacation!

I focused on the bone in the middle of Gayl's breasts to keep standing, to take it, her punch, her laugh. She saw where I was looking.

'Check it out, Elijah. She's different from the rest.'

I was starting to get it, even though I could barely see. I was being punched. I was equal with her now. I didn't move my eyes from that bone in the middle of her body, her heart was somewhere under there. I was starting to get what was going on: I was being slapped and punched into being by a slapped and punched being. I needed to be cracked, the protection I was born with.

Elijah took the camera away from his face. 'I think we got enough,' he said.

'She needs more,' Gayl said, forcing me to focus. 'This one needs more.'

Gayl stopped swaying. I was able to look at her face. It was beat-up and startling. We looked in each other's eyes.

Gayl lifted her arm back in the air.

'Do it,' I heard coming out of my mouth. I was revolting.

Gayl smiled. I smiled. She opened her fist. She turned her hand around so I could see her cracked and raised knuckles. I lifted my chin up in the air. I could take her backwards slap. My whole world was changing.

'This is it.'

The backwards blow made me split right in half. I saw the world how it was meant to be seen: broken and freaked, full of masters and slaves. Elijah and Gayl came from circumstances of hardship and I came from circumstances of ease. The knowledge of hardship is not as easily passed on as the knowledge of ease. Gayl had smacked me awake and the whole world could see.

Suddenly, I felt her arms around me. Hair and dread was all over my face. A body of sun came into the room through a crack in the drapes.

'Get this for the end,' I heard Gayl whisper to Elijah. She was hugging me, smoothing my hair. 'I know this is different, E., but get this for the end.'

Our reconciliation would come across in the film: the snuff film of my consciousness.

LEE: God. I want to hold her. Fucking hell. It's illegal. This is child porn.

GAYL: Child porn? Yeah? People do this all over the world.

LEE: You call yourself an artist?

GAYL: I am an artist.

LEE: You make child porn.

GAYL: Nah, come on, Lee. Use your brain. This is not child porn. You know it's not that. Myra isn't working. She's sixteen. She knows she's onstage.

LEE: She's seventeen. So what?

GAYL: I make liberation porn. All my actors get that. They come to me for that. They follow me for that. You get it? It's the opposite of child porn.

LEE: The opposite. What's the fucking opposite of child porn?

GAYL: You just saw it. And check out all my work, lady: www.hotkentuckizianporn.com

§

My father staggered when he saw me. He went from dull eyes to abnormally sparked.

'I'm fine.' I stood at the doorway to the kitchen, hand up to fend him off. 'I'm totally fine.'

A woman with a mop in her arms stared too. It was Anna from Indonesia. Younger than my mother, no folds on her face.

'Myra, I will go to the police, and if you think I won't …'

My father didn't even know why he was saying the police, but my punched-out jaw and slapped cheeks must have made it seem to make sense. 'Your face, Myra. Oh my god. What happened to you?'

'I'm fine,' I said again, softer. 'My face heals quickly, remember? I promise that it's fine.'

My father didn't go down to the basement. He climbed up the stairs to my parents' old room. I was still and so was Anna until we heard a door shut.

'Come,' Anna said from the corner of the kitchen.

I followed her to the side door of the pantry. She opened a large red leather bag. I sat down on the floor and closed my eyes. Anna didn't say anything as she rubbed some kind of cream into my jaw that smelled like milk past its date.

Then she made me ginger tea, to bring down the swelling, she said. She was quiet and compact and kind.

When my father came back downstairs, I was drinking the tea and Anna was cleaning the counter.

'Do you want to go visit your mother? We can put it on my points.'

'I don't want to,' I said.

'But it's not working. This isn't working.'

'What isn't?'

'This. You're having problems. We can all see that.'

My father was trying to formulate a plan.

'So maybe you living here isn't working anymore.' His father's voice caught. He looked over at Anna. It occurred to me that my father was looking to Anna for support. 'I think you should try something else. Another school. You're not attending.'

'I am! I'm almost finished my final paper!' It hurt my jaw to exclaim. 'I just have to finish the conclusion, all right?'

Anna crouched down underneath the sink.

'I still think you should go visit your mother. Myra, I don't know what to do anymore.'

'You know my mother's staying at a love hotel, right?'

'I'm not interested in that.'

'She's teaching businessmen how to read.'

'Good. Good for her.'

'She says that Asia is the new Europe and she's going to backpack around Thailand and Indonesia for a while with her new friends. Maybe Anna has some pointers for her about the locals. She could probably use them. You're from Indonesia, right, Anna?'

'I said, Myra, we don't want to know.'

'We?'

My father put his face in his hands. He made a few half-coughing sounds.

There were pictures in photo albums stacked in our basement of my father holding all of us as babies, first Jody, then me, then Jeff. He held us all up in the air over his head and we flew. He looked happy in those pictures with his skinny arms straight up. He was able to make us laugh. I didn't understand how that father was the same person as this one.

Anna held a yellow plastic bottle of dish cleaner in one hand. She went over to my father and handed him a tissue. My father looked at me, embarrassed. He took the tissue.

'Thank you,' he said. 'Thank you, Anna.'

'I'm not going to visit my mother,' I said. 'I mean, I don't want to go.'

'Okay,' my dad said. 'Then we're going to the hospital.'

'No!' Anna yelled.

Anna looked at me straight. I looked at my father. I didn't blame him that he thought he should take me to the hospital to find out what was going on. But it felt like Anna understood where I got my beat-up face: in a learning position.

'See, Dad? It's okay, I'm fine, Anna agrees.'

'You're not fine. Fucking hell. Excuse me.'

Me and my dad stood there like that, both our chests caving in while Anna was back at the sink, scrubbing a pot, and then at the fridge hauling out plastic bags. I didn't know where all that food came from. Eventually, Anna looked at my dad and smiled as encouragement.

'Anna's making dinner tonight. Tofu goreng. Do you want to eat with us? Jeff is joining us too. Jody might arrive a bit later because she's coming in for the weekend.'

'Since when do you eat tofu?' Since when does a domestic worker make our dinners?

'Anna shared her lunch with me a few times,' my father said.

After you deleted your stash of bikini-fisted cunts? Anna chopped garlic. My father looked at the floor. I wanted to laugh but no laughs would come.

'After all these years your mother just couldn't do it anymore,' my dad said. 'Your mother and I are getting a divorce. I still have to tell Jeff that this is final. But you know that, correct?'

My father rubbed his face. Anna, with sticky hands, was beside him again with a fresh tissue, like a saviour, or a moth. I wasn't babying him like my mother thought. But he needed babying, it seemed. And my mother was out of that role, a millionaire now. She'd just sent me and Jeff a package in the mail. It had two Korean bank envelopes inside, one for him and one for me. The envelopes said *Korean Kash for my Kids! Kiss, Kiss!* in a weird loopy script that I didn't recognize. Each of our envelopes had two thousand bucks in American bills.

'*Myra*. You know that your mother and I are getting a divorce, correct?'

I had two thousand American dollars courtesy of my mother's revolt.

Anna was back at the garlic, chopping. Her skin seemed moist, her black eyes were bright.

'I know that Spartacus was the leader of a slave revolution,' I said. 'I know that slaves rise up and fight.'

My father looked scared of me. Anna, eyes down, did not.

'Come on, Dad. *Yes*. I know that, yes. Divorce, correct. I'll come for dinner. Thank you, Anna.'

My father's face settled. It was as if, for one second, he understood my need for spectacle.

§

In my bedroom, healing, I read Aaron's Weil. The floors shone, the sheets were clean because of Anna. 'Subordination: economy of energy. Thanks to this, an act of heroism can be performed without there being any need for the person who commands or the one who obeys to be a hero.'

Lee called me the moment I moved from Weil to Bataille.

'I know you didn't want me to talk to your father,' Lee said. 'I know I crossed that line.'

I read from Bataille in silence: *Cruelty and eroticism are conscious intentions in a mind which has resolved to trespass into a forbidden field of behaviour.*

'Myra? Respond. Talk, please. I'm sorry.'

It was my conscious intention to trespass into a forbidden field of behaviour.

'Look, I just feel like since I kept what happened to me from my parents for so long, I'm really sensitive to it,' Lee said. 'I'm kind of on the side of the parents.'

'You were in Grade 6, Lee. I am seventeen years old.'

'I *know*, Myra. That's why I'm saying I'm sorry. I miss you. I'm sorry. I'm just overprotective. You're working it out, I know. I don't want our friendship to be aborted in the process. You're just in this really raw state of something unreal … '

My heart sped up. Lee didn't understand. Pornography with Gayl and Elijah was *real*. It was my forbidden field to stomp in – full of hairy red flowers on sharp spotted stalks.

'Myra? *You* still exist, okay? *You're* real.'

'Listen to this.' I cracked open the centre of the book, a section of Bataille that I had never read before: '"*Silence cannot do away with things that language cannot state. Violence is as stub-bornly there just as much as death, and if language cheats to conceal universal annihilation, the placid work of time, language alone suffers.'"* I paused on that, repeating: *"'Language alone suffers, language is the poorer, not time and not violence.'"* Hey, Lee, you think I can finish my essay in language that does not suffer?'

'No. I don't.'

'Why?'

'Myra, listen, I want to be friends with *you*, okay?' Lee said softly. 'The free woman, the tender one, not the one in thrall of some violent American asshole and his girlfriend.'

'Elijah is Tanzanian and Gayl is from Kentucky,' I said quickly. I was anticipating sex: violence, assholes, annihilation. 'Gayl is really smart. She's an artist. I think you should meet her.'

'They're using you.'

'They are not.'

'Of course they are.'

'I don't care if they are.'

'You *should* care, Myra.'

But I didn't. I had money in my pocket. I had a thick enve-lope of cash. I wanted to see Gayl and Elijah with my money, with my freedom, and explode on the floor, come on the floor, show my tits tongue ass and knees to both of them together. I wanted to share the money from my mother. Somehow the whole thing made sense. Slave revolt cash for a slave revolting.

'Myra?'

'What.'

'What are you thinking right now?'

I wasn't thinking. I was shaking. Language cheats and conceals. 'I am on this path of Absolute Knowledge,' I whispered.

Lee didn't respond. We were both silent for a while.

Then she said, 'Bataille does not believe in Absolute Knowl-edge, you know.'

I didn't know.

'Wait, just hang on.'

I heard her go through the pages of a book. 'Okay here it is: "*Circular absolute knowledge is definitive non-knowledge*," Lee read slowly, each word intense. 'That is Bataille, okay? True inner experience can't be mapped by absolutes. The whole Hegelian thing was too neat for him. Bataille was all about the cracks. Myra?'

The cracks? Knowledge is cracky? Was it hairy too? I started laughing. It hurt my jaw to laugh. Was cracky, hairy, uncertain knowledge the key to getting fucked a thousand times? Or was it the key to making annihilating porn with a violent asshole and an artist? Or was there no key to any of this?

'Myra, let me come over there,' Lee said. 'I really feel like laughing with you.'

'But my face is fucked up. It hurts to laugh.'

'What's wrong with your face?'

'Black eyes. A red jaw.'

'God, Myra. *Fuck*. I was right.'

'You're right. Bataille is right. I'm not suffering. I just have to write it down.'

'Let me come over.'

'No. Not now.'

'*Please*, Myra. Let me.'

'I have to write. I have to finish my essay.'

I heard Lee breathing loudly into the phone. I didn't know if she was angry or worried or what.

'Why don't you come for dinner later? Anna's making tofu goreng. Jody's coming home. It smells pretty good in here. All right?'

It was three o'clock in the afternoon. I would act out my conclusion. Come home half-formed, tail dragging: free.

'Myra ... '

'Yeah?'

'Who's Anna?'

'My father's slave.'

§

The Y-shaped gold handle on Room 303 was stuck. It had a safety pin sticking out of the centre. It wouldn't open for me. I banged on the door.

Gayl answered. She was alert, her shoulders pinned to her back, her back straight.

'Sunny,' she said, eyeing me. ''Tis a brand-new day.'

I had two thousand dollars in my pocket. 'It is, yeah.'

I walked in past her. Gayl watched me. She could tell I was confident.

'You heal pretty good,' she said, shutting the door and pressing her body up against it.

Anna had served me cup after cup of tea while I wrote. She kept knocking like a little bird on my bedroom door. I kept thanking her and thanking her, saying, no more! That's enough! Thank you, Anna! Now only my left cheek was still puffy. My eyes had a yellowish-violet tint around them. That's all.

'To tell you the truth,' Gayl said, 'I'm surprised we're even fucking seeing you again.'

Gayl's eyes were as bruised as the day before. She sat down at the table where there was an opened can of kidney beans.

'Yeah? Well, don't be surprised,' I said. I felt tall in my body. I pushed out my chest and smiled. I felt excited to be with her. I was here, consciously, loaded with cash and the desire not to conceal violence. I had concluded my thinking on the slave.

'Men don't like to see the marks they make,' Gayl said.

'Oh no?' I smiled.

Gayl smiled back at me. I think we both had the same thought: sometimes *everyone* wants to see what they've done.

'Where's Elijah?' I asked.

'Elijah is gone.'

'Where?'

'You don't know?'

I got nervous all of a sudden. Where was he? I wanted the three of us. I wanted our porn.

Gayl stared at me. She made a pulse start in my cheek.

I fiddled around in my purse for my stash. I had only enough for one joint. But there was a perfect little pebble of hash stuck to some papers at the bottom of my bag. Aaron must've slipped it to me at some point without me knowing.

'You think that's going to make it better?' Gayl asked.

'I hope it's still good,' I said quickly, passing her the hash. 'It's been in my purse for a while.'

Gayl turned on the hot plate. She shoved a butter knife between the coils. The curtains were open. Bronze squares flashed into the room. I thought of dinner with Lee and Anna, my dad, Jody and Jeff. It would be better than Gayl's kidney beans. I imagined her around our table too.

'My customers liked you,' Gayl said. 'They want to see more of you soon.'

'Okay.' Another session was what I wanted. A chance to work with her again, be with him.

Gayl pressed a piece of hash on the back of a spoon. Then she slipped the blackened knife out of the burner and smashed the two utensils together. She sucked in the thick smoke like she did it every day, staring at me the whole time.

'I was taught not to lie, Myra,' she said at the top of her breath. 'I was taught by my mummy to tell the whole truth.'

I wasn't lying. I had tried in my essay not to lie. I'd tried to write in language that did not suffer. *It doesn't matter*, I wrote, *if the slave is ashamed, or takes pleasure, or displays themselves in pornography. It does not matter if their lack of freedom is traumatic or experiential. Because the self-conscious narrative of the slave*, I concluded, *is a liberation narrative.*

Gayl was holding her breath, holding in the hash.

'That stuff is really strong,' I said.

Gayl coughed out her smoke and laughed in hoarse barks. 'You're getting used to our high-art bullshit already?'

'Yeah, I am,' I said. What's the problem with that?

Gayl put the knife back into the coil for another hit. She set it up quick and sucked in a funnel of smoke.

I was basically committing myself to being in her films.

The slave revolt is a leap into the unknown, I wrote, *into Bataillean non-knowledge, into direct, definitive confrontation with the power of the master that has defined the slave, defined the slave in her innocence. Because the slave also defines the master. The loop of the master and slave thus cannot be closed. It is open, repeating, electrically charged. This is the narrative structure of liberation: a possibility of non-identification with oneself – how one was born, how one wakes up – either master or slave. Because you can be fucked a thousand times and still be a virgin.*

'We're only here for a little while longer,' Gayl said at the top of her breath, holding out the smoking knife and spoon for me to take her remnants. I leaned over the table to take it in. 'But you know that, Miss World Traveller, don't you?'

I held in my smoke. No, I didn't know that.

'You're an explorer who flaps her legs open like a book.'

Smoke exploded from Gayl's nose. She was a dragon, red-eyed, dominant. I felt my mother-money in my pocket like a weapon.

I had emailed my essay to Ms. Bain and Mr. Rotowsky. I'd emailed Chris, Lee and Aaron a copy too. I'd even sent one to Jen and Charlene. *Girls*, I wrote, *wrestle with this!*

Gayl set up our last hit of hash. Her forehead protruded and shone like a dome. 'Once you started, you just couldn't stop, right? Once you started you got so open that you'd do anything.'

'Yeah, that's it,' I said. 'That's what happened to me.'

Gayl offered the last hit to me. 'I hear him call you our little bourgie bitch,' she said.

'Fuck you,' I said. I felt like Lee.

I half stood up to reach for Gayl's arm over the table. Then I held her there and sucked. I wasn't afraid of anything anymore.

'You aren't so young, Myra, but sometimes you really seem young. Like, maybe twelve, not seventeen.'

Our faces were close. Gayl was scrambling or something, her eyes were glossy. When you're eighteen you can do whatever you want, I wanted to say. My mother got married when she was nineteen. I felt my waist in the edge of the table. My mother gave me this shitload of cash. I was on the verge of showing my money to her. Sharing. Gayl's mouth opened. Her swollen eyes closed.

Gayl had seen me and made me do things that I wanted. I breathed my smoke out into her mouth. Her lips opened wide and easy.

But Gayl extracted her wrist from my grip and went to lie down on the bed. The smock she was wearing rode up around her waist. Gayl had on see-through yellow underwear.

'Camera,' she said, pointing.

The burlap bag was by the wall. The room felt webbed up with smoke. The camera in the sack was heavy and plastic, all its cords twisted up.

'It's already charged,' Gayl said quietly.

My body was shaky with hash. I looked through the eye. I pressed the red little button on the side.

Gayl was in a goddess position. An exposure position.

She pulled aside and pinned back her underwear. She had short black hairs around her cunt like the ring of an eclipse. A part of her down there looked way too red, how my face had been red from Key West, burning alive.

I filmed her until the tape ran out. My eyes went blurry behind the camera. Gayl closed her legs and her eyes. I put down the camera. It was six o'clock. It was time for me to go.

'Don't leave,' Gayl whispered. She looked so sleepy. 'You can be my little helper.'

'I'll come back,' I said. 'I'll be back tomorrow.'

It was weird, for a moment, to leave her there alone on the bed.

'He'd be so disappointed if I let you go now,' Gayl said. 'The bitch got away. Our little bourgie bitch.'

The door was locked, it was locked from the outside. I rattled it back and forth to get out. I remembered that safety pin in the handle. I don't know how long I was there at the door not wanting to realize that we were locked in. It was on purpose.

When I turned around, Gayl was back at the table.

'I have to be home for dinner.'

'Home for dinner!' Gayl laughed. 'This is happening, so you just better sit.'

I didn't want to miss Anna's dinner with Jeff and my dad, with Jody and Lee. I must've look panicked. Gayl was tracing the veins on the back of her hand, her worker's hand.

'He was disappointed, you know, that you weren't so rich.'

I wanted to call my dad. They couldn't keep me in here.

'Myra, man, it's the way of the world!'

I took my money out of my pocket.

'Yeah, you people travel from wish to wish and want to want. You people think that the world is a playground.'

'How do you know what kind of person I am?' I said, holding my two-thousand-dollar-stuffed envelope. 'You don't even know me!'

Gayl slammed her hands so hard into the table that one leg collapsed. The hot plate shifted.

'Did you have your own bedroom growing up?'

My body felt skewered like the table.

'Myra, sit the fuck back down.'

I did not sit back down. I wanted to stand.

'I slept on the floor with four brothers.' Gayl said, looking up at me. 'Head to foot and foot to head.'

Could the house I grew up in reduce me to this? I stared down at Gayl, at the clear space on her forehead between her eyes.

'We don't have this desire to be like you, Myra. I don't, at least.'

I knew she wasn't saying this stuff to make me feel bad.

Behind Gayl was the window that faced the sky. The air was now murky and uniform.

I put my mother's envelope down on the table.

Gayl clamped her hand on top of it. 'Thank you,' she said. She knew exactly what was inside.

Gayl took my envelope over to the window and pulled down the blinds. I had stayed standing, tall.

'I'm going to sleep now,' Gayl said. 'You want to be in the bed with me or what?'

I knew that Lee would be freaked and my dad would be freaked that I wasn't at home. I thought they would ransack my computer and find all my porn.

A streetcar shrieked on the road, its headlights flashed under the blind. Maybe I did want to be in the bed with her.

'He shouldn't be able to do that to you,' I said.

Gayl didn't look at me. She got into bed. I watched her twist herself up in the sheets, settle down. I waited for a click, a sound from the door. I thought of Lee and Wils, Aaron and Chris, Jen and Charlene, Ms. Bain and Mr. Rotowsky, all reading my paper on the liberation of the slave. I walked to the bed and stood over Gayl. Sensing me, she turned out the covers.

'How come you stay with him?' I whispered.

Gayl reached up for me.

'It's a mystery,' she said.

I climbed in there with her. Her arm swung over my shoulder, landed on my neck. It was fiery. I couldn't fall asleep. She smelled like coins and smoke and blood.

§

A grey sheet hung and stuck on my face. My back was twisted. I woke up under the three-legged table. One of the sheets from the bed had been placed on top of me. An electric-blue crack lit under the blinds. I was all bruised. I didn't know why I was on the floor.

Elijah and Gayl were in the same bed, the bed I'd been in. Gayl held Elijah, his humpback knotted with nodes for the spine. The first time I saw him, he was sweating on the beach, cracked grey toes and a walking stick. I was the stranger in this room. I thought about the door. I walked to the door.

Please please please let there not be a lock anymore.

Please please please let there not be a lock.

'You are not leaving with your money, little bitch.'

My master was standing behind me, way too close. *Bitch* had lost its meaning now.

'What?' I said. I did not turn around.

What? is not a plan, Lee would've said.

What? was weakness, according to Gayl.

'Come back to bed now.' Elijah grabbed my upper arm.

'Everyone knows where I am,' I said.

Elijah tightened his grip on me. 'Doesn't matter. Turn around. I want to see you.'

I knew Elijah was naked and spectacular. I didn't turn around. He blocked me with his body against the door.

'Let me go,' I said quietly. 'She has the money.'

'I really like you.' Elijah put his lips to my ear. He bit my earlobe. I felt my knees hit the door. 'Don't you like me, Angel? I like you, don't you like me?'

I turned my head and we started kissing. My stomach cramped. Elijah's mouth was on my mouth, his tongue moved inside and he kept pressing up into my body with his whole body.

'You have my money,' I said between breaths. 'I just want to leave now. Please.'

'You don't want to leave. Look at you. You're burning up, baby.'

I couldn't stop myself from kissing him. Elijah had my whole head. His hand snaked and forced up between my body and the door. 'Please, please, god, please.' I heard myself, desperate. I couldn't stop myself from doing what we were doing.

There was a truck outside, the garbage being dumped.

'Our slave's not so willing anymore,' Gayl said. She was naked behind Elijah. She saw right through me.

'It doesn't matter.'

Elijah's fingers slipped inside me. The door vibrated. I pushed down in my legs for more. Noise expanded. I got slammed in the face. Elijah yelled. I didn't feel him anymore. The door pushed us all down. A woman led me to the wall. Gayl got hit by two men in black gloves. Four cops had Elijah, who fought them off, spitting. His hair was shaking. He tried to find me. They locked his hands behind his back. They put a sheet over his head. Gayl was caped with one of the sheets. She was not shocked, arms behind her like him. She still had her eyes. We stared at each other.

Six cops led them out of the room: tied up, foreign, liberation done.

I'd met Elijah alone on the beach. Gayl had changed the look of me forever. Our meeting was the first in a chain of events that the expansion of my consciousness was built on.

'Your father is waiting in a car outside for you,' the policewoman said. She wore glasses that magnified the whites of her eyes.

A few guys in suits were undoing the room. They dumped out three burlap sacks that were stashed in the closet. Small black tapes scattered on the used mattress – the animal shit of the camera's corpse.

§

My father sat beside me in carpeted rooms. Police held lukewarm cups of tea. My dad held my hand. They'd all seen the way me and Elijah had sex. *Young Canadian Caught up in African Porn Ring*. That's how it was told in the paper, minor unnamed. My fantasies were elucidated for the masses.

Elijah and Gayl had been deported. Gayl to Lexington and Elijah to Dar es Salaam. Dar es Salaam means Haven of Peace. The cops said that the Americans and the Africans would have to deal with their garbage. The cops gave some psychiatrist's number to my dad. Everyone wanted my rehabilitation. They'd all seen how I'd taken those blows, the way I hid myself after in the heart of the director.

GAYL: She hid herself in me but I was no place to hide.

LEE: Why did you want to destroy her like this?

GAYL: Destroy? What are you talking about? Who do you think was destroyed? I'm the one who's locked up now. I'm the one who can't have a life. I'm the one who has to sit on my ass and write letters of confession.

LEE: Well, maybe some of that will be healing, or whatever.

GAYL: Healing? I don't think so. I'd prefer my pussy get healed. It misses being fucked. Who's got something for me there?

§

I was naked lying on top of my covers. Lee stood at the doorway of my bedroom trying to convince me to come with her and Wils and Aaron to Aaron's parents' place in Florida. She said that we could rent a car and go off on adventures by ourselves.

'Bataille says that the power of the abject is the hunger for strong sensations,' I said. 'To feel yourself alive in the face of abomination.'

Lee entered my room and sat on the floor. 'Bataille's for boys.'

I could not do anything to free Elijah, to free Gayl. I wasn't going to talk to any psychiatrist. Ms. Bain and Mr. Rotowsky did not give my essay an A or A plus. They gave me a joint and mutual C. *With reservations*, they wrote. *This is all over the place. Please be careful of being too personal in your writing.*

'Did you know that Chris had a major crush on you?' Lee said.

'Why're you changing the subject?'

'I'm not.'

'You are. And he did not have a crush on me. He hated me.'

'He told me he could barely look at you the first time he met you. He told me he thought you were the most beautiful girl he had ever seen. He was totally turned on by your thinking. He still wants to publish your piece. He says to thank you for sending it, he loves the new version. You should give him a call. Tell him yes or no. About the piece, I mean.' Lee smiled at me.

I felt myself smile back at her even though I didn't want to be smiling.

§

Anna dumped out the mop bucket in the kitchen sink. The water was elephant-coloured, a gush of torn nails and hairs. She was telling me about her three grown-up kids in Indonesia. Anna had been working in Canada since the kids were little and she had a sixteen-year-old at home, the baby she'd left with her own mother right after she'd been born. Anna had flown on a plane to Saudi Arabia one week after giving birth to her youngest. Anna said that working motivated her. She said that she cried for twenty-four hours straight after leaving her baby, but then she never cried about it again. The baby's name was Innalo. Innalo would be going to university because of the money that Anna sent home over sixteen years every single week and Anna said that this was worth it. For not knowing her daughter at all, it was worth it that she, alone, would go to university. Anna said that my father had been very, very good to her, better than any family she had ever worked for in sixteen years. She told me that my father had offered to sponsor Innalo to come live in Canada so that she could study at a Canadian university.

'You kids are lucky,' Anna said. 'To have such a good and responsible man as your dad.'

Anna smoothed out and folded our plastic bags. 'Some ladies commit suicide,' she said, 'on the path that I have taken.'

§

I had a video camera in front of my face, shooting my friends as I told them a story: 'Gayl filmed girls being fucked for the first time,' the story started. 'White virgins, Western virgins seduced by a beautiful and perverted Tanzanian musician. Then, for this totally spectacular ending, Gayl filmed the girls getting beat up by her.'

The sun was strong in Fort Lauderdale. I wasn't positive if my ending was the only ending like that, or not. If I was the only one who was turned free by that violence, or not. Aaron's parents had a huge fancy place with a pool. All of Gayl's footage and archives had been destroyed.

'It was this totally backwards and inspired allegory about masters and slaves,' I continued. 'Gayl was trying to make the masters aware of their privilege, the people who wouldn't ever think of themselves as masters. A master can be a total innocent, you know, just from where she was born, how she grew up.'

I'd talked to my mom for a long time on the phone in Aaron's parents' bedroom suite. She said that people in Korea had been calling her Nina, not Irene.

'Gayl made this kind of dialectical porn that degraded the oppressors.' Lee and Aaron and Wils watched me, rapt. I had them. I could keep them. 'Gayl made this porn to fuck up the people watching it, the people paying for it. She wanted to take these people to the height of their fantasy and give them what they wanted to see, like a teenage slut getting fucked, full of depravity and need, but then right at the moment of orgasm she could subvert the whole equation.'

'How?' asked Lee. 'That's what I want to know.'

'She got me, playing slut-slave, to embrace her, my female oppressor. The man as the perverse force was negated onscreen in the self-consciousness that all of us were actors.'

I imagined Nina in Korea in her love hotel, full of money and bursting, a whole other world.

'I've been committed to tape,' I told my friends in Florida. 'I believe in what I've done. I don't regret a thing. That's what porn is. It's sharing yourself.'

Lee smiled at me, she licked the salt off her glass. It was a good shot. Aaron and Wils were our witnesses.

'Sharing is pleasure is lack of regret,' said Lee. 'I think we think we all agree.'

Notes

Epigraph: *The dream of all men is to meet little sluts who are innocent but ready for all forms of depravity – which is what, more or less, all teenage girls are.* Michel Houellebecq, from *The Possibility of an Island*, p. 144. First Vintage International Edition, 2007

Epigraph: *My mystery is that I have no mystery.* Clarice Lispector from *Why This World: A Biography of Clarice Lispector* by Benjamin Moser. p. 4. New York: Oxford University Press, 2009

p. 11, 122, 125, 157: *You could be raped a thousand times and you could still be a virgin.* From an email to the author from Moritz Gaede

p. 48: *I am Myra Breckinridge, whom no man will ever possess.* Gore Vidal, the opening line of *Myra Breckinridge*, New York: Bantam, 1968

p. 62: *Love is a sign of our wretchedness, God can only love himself. We can only love something else.* Simone Weil from *Gravity and Grace*, p. 62. London: Routledge Classics, 2002

p. 90: *Shame is the most proper emotive tonality of subjectivity.* Giorgio Agamben from *Remnants of Auschwitz*, p. 110. New York: Zone Books, 2002

p. 122: *Is it right to ignore me like this as if they did nothing to me? Were the soldiers justified in trampling an innocent and fragile teenage girl and making her suffer for the rest of her life?* A paraphrase of Miss Kim from the article 'Inside Queens: The Memories of a Comfort Woman,' by Jane H. Lii, published September 10, 1995, in the *New York Times*

p. 125: *Base feelings, envy, resentment are degraded energy.* Simone Weil from *Gravity and Grace*, p. 8

p. 136: *A test of what is real is that it is hard and rough. Joys are found in it, not pleasure. What is pleasant belongs to dreams.* Simone Weil from *Gravity and Grace*, p. 53

p. 152: *Subordination: economy of energy. Thanks to this, an act of heroism can be performed without there being any need for the person who commands or the one who obeys to be a hero.* Simone Weil from *Gravity and Grace*, p. 43

p. 152: *Cruelty and eroticism are conscious intentions in a mind which has resolved to trespass into a forbidden field of behaviour.* Georges Bataille from *Eroticism*, p. 80. London: Penguin Books, 2001

p. 152–3: *Silence cannot do away with things that language cannot state. Violence is as stubbornly there just as much as death, and if language cheats to conceal universal annihilation, the placid work of time, language alone suffers, language is the poorer, not time and not violence.* Georges Bataille from *Eroticism*, p. 187

p. 154: *Circular absolute knowledge is definitive non-knowledge.* Georges Bataille from *Inner Experience*, p. 108. New York: State University of New York Press, 1988

p. 163: *The power of the abject is the hunger for strong sensations. To feel yourself alive in the face of abomination.* Myra paraphrasing Georges Bataille, from *Eroticism*

Acknowledgements

Thank you to Rachel Fulford, Tess Chakkalakal, Emily Pohl-Weary, Susan Winemaker, Rosa Pagano, Lise Soskolne, Moritz Gaede, Christine Davis, Allen Forbes and Kika Thorne for talking with me about this book at various points of its existence.

Thanks to the Ontario Arts Council for a Works in Progress grant.

Thank you immeasurably to my editor, Alana Wilcox.

Thank you to Evan Munday and Leigh Nash for working on behalf of this book.

Thank you to Sam Hiyate and to Sarah Williams for working with me on early drafts.

Thank you to Geraldine Bowman, Sheldon Berger, Randie Berger, Ari Berger, Wolf Virgo and especially Clement Virgo, my family.

About the Author

Tamara Faith Berger was born in Toronto. She wrote porn stories for a living and attempted to make dirty films before publishing her first book, *Lie with Me*, in 1999. In 2001, *The Way of the Whore* (*A Woman Alone at Night* in the U.S.), her second book, was published. In 2004, *Lie with Me* was made into a film. *Maidenhead* is her third book.

Typeset in Whitman

Printed at the old Coach House on bpNichol Lane in Toronto, Ontario, on Zephyr Antique Laid paper, which was manufactured, acid-free, in Saint-Jérôme, Quebec, from second-growth forests. This book was printed with vegetable-based ink on a 1965 Heidelberg KORD offset litho press. Its pages were folded on a Baumfolder, gathered by hand, bound on a Sulby Auto-Minabinda and trimmed on a Polar single-knife cutter.

Edited and designed by Alana Wilcox
Cover design and hand-lettering by Ingrid Paulson
Author photograph by Christine Davis

Coach House Books
80 bpNichol Lane
Toronto ON M5S 3J4
Canada

416 979 2217
800 367 6360

mail@chbooks.com
www.chbooks.com